Donovan Trait is a marked man. He is flamboyant, stunningly handsome, and notoriously insatiable, but his attitude and style belie his skills in the courtroom. No one survives a cross-examination at Donovan's hands. His knowledge of the law and trial practice has accumulated over the years . . . and years, of experience. More than three hundred years. You see, when Donovan isn't seducing judges and juries, he's a creature of the night. And now that someone has decided that it's time to kill all lawyers, his lust for attention has set him in the murderer's sights.

The problem is that vampires don't die. Not easily, anyway. That's good news for Donovan, not so much for his very human lady love, also a target of the serial killer. Will several unsuccessful attempts on his life expose Donovan's true nature? Will the killer learn the secret that will guarantee a permanent death? Or will Donovan finally manage to put an end to the killer's murderous spree and live happily ever after, with his lady love?

First, We Kill All the Lawyers

ISBN: 978-1-4874-3126-6
Cover art by Martine Jardin



Published by eXtasy Books Inc or
Devine Destinies, an imprint of eXtasy Books Inc

Look for us online at:
www.eXtasybooks.com or www.devinedestinies.com

# First, We Kill All the Lawyers
## Donovan Trait 1

By

Seelie Kay

# Dedication

*To friends and family who have reached across cultural, racial, and religious lines for love.*

# Chapter One: A Recusal for Love

Donovan Trait whipped off his designer trench coat and, with a quick smile at the judge, neatly draped it over the bar separating the gallery from the court.

He adjusted his cuffs, smoothed his suit coat, and tweaked a crease in his slacks. Then his lips curled up into a grin. "My apologies, Your Honor," he said with his classic aristocratic flair, just a hint of a British accent clipping his vowels. "The elevated commuter train was held up by some unfathomable crisis." He shrugged. "I thought that would get me across town faster than a cab, but once again, I was proved wrong. I've been on trains across the Midwest, delayed by cows or sheep, even the occasional misguided commuter, but the El just leaves me flummoxed. It seems to stop whenever, for only God knows whatever reason." Donovan brushed a lock of hair off his forehead and smirked. "My paralegal calls them El-Farts."

Those in the courtroom chuckled. The judge, however, scowled. Shirley Magnusen narrowed her clear blue eyes and pointed her gavel at Donovan. "Why do I think you were late because you were forced to tear yourself away from the arms of some blonde bimbo providing you with afternoon delights?" Her stern gaze swept his body. Then she chuckled and shook her head. She patted her blonde hair, pulled back into a neat bun, and her ruby red lips rewarded him with a sly smile. "Not sure why you were named one of Chicago's most eligible bachelors. I don't see the attraction at all, but your many trysts are no excuse for being late to court." She pointed her gavel at him. "Don't let it happen again."

Donovan placed a hand over his heart. "Your Honor, you wound me. I merely got a late start this morning and I have been unable to catch up. Please be assured that I hurried to this court in great anticipation of . . ."

District Attorney Wallace J. Sullivan cleared his throat. "Your Honor, must the rest of us be subjected to this bull . . . um, malarkey? Unlike defense counsel, I take my job seriously, and I would like to proceed. I have defendants to hang, witnesses to fry." He chuckled. "And I so enjoy inflicting my legal prowess on Attorney Trait." He plucked at the arm of his suit coat as if removing a piece of lint, a smile blooming on his face. "Like taking candy from a baby."

Judge Magnusen nodded. "Alright. Let's begin." She gestured to Donovan. "Counselor Trait. I believe you have a motion or two?"

Donovan winked at her. "Of course, I do, Your Honor. Where would you like to begin?"

The judge rolled her eyes. "At the beginning, Counselor. Now get on with it. Unlike the El, this court has a schedule, and we stick to it."

Donovan bowed his head in deference. "Of course, Your Honor." He pulled a legal pad from his briefcase and studied it for a moment. Then he gazed at the judge, a slight smile crossing his face. "Your Honor, I move for a complete dismissal of the charges against my client. With prejudice, of course."

Judge Magnusen frowned. "On what grounds?"

Donovan shook his head, trying to appear dismayed. "Sadly, Your Honor, on the grounds of illegal search and seizure. A violation of the Fourth Amendment to the U.S. Constitution and Article I, Section Six of the Illinois State Constitution, which states . . ."

The judge waved her hand. "I know what it says,

Counselor. Let's get down to the nitty-gritty."

"Of course, Your Honor. The police had no arrest or search warrant when they broke down my client's door. They didn't even have probable cause to enter. Their entire conversation before entering the premises revolved around whether their search warrant would come through in time to conduct a legal search. They also failed to knock and announce before entering. Instead, they just barged in and seized everything they could find."

The D.A. huffed and muttered, "He's making that up."

Donovan went back to his briefcase and pulled out a rectangular device. He held it up for the judge to see. "It was all recorded on my client's doorbell, Your Honor. This little doorbell has sound and sight capabilities. I believe it is called *A Ring*. My client called me while the police were discussing their options. I advised him to let them implicate themselves. I also told him to demand a warrant, and when they couldn't produce one, to deny them entry."

Sullivan jumped to his feet. "Your Honor, we were not made aware of this evidence." In a haughty tone, he added. "Besides, you cannot record people without their permission. That evidence is inadmissible."

The judge scowled and peered over her reading glasses at the District Attorney. "Nice try, Wally. Security tapes used to prove or disprove an alleged crime arc always admissiblc and you know it. Now let the counselor proceed."

"Thank you, Your Honor." Donovan approached the bench and handed the judge a document. "As this transcript reveals, the police knew they were entering illegally." He walked over to Sullivan and tossed a copy to him. "Then the District Attorney attempted to cover their blunder by claiming the evidence they seized was in plain sight, rendering the seizure legal." Donovan turned toward the judge and scratched his head. "I don't know where our esteemed D.A.

studied law, but at Harvard, we were taught that an illegal entry makes anything seized thereafter *the fruit of the poisonous tree.*

"Which means, of course, that all the evidence used to arrest and indict my client was inadmissible. And that means none of the resulting charges can stand.

"I respectfully request dismissal of all charges against my client, with prejudice." Donovan gazed at the District Attorney, his expression stern. "I also ask that all evidence seized illegally be returned to my client forthwith." Donovan removed another sheet of paper from his briefcase. "My client's wife recorded every single item seized. Not only did she manually maintain an inventory, but it was also verified with an in-home security camera. We will consider any cash or valuables missing from that inventory to have been the subject of theft, at the hands of the police or the D.A.'s office." He handed the list to the judge and smirked. "My client will not stand for sticky fingers, Your Honor. He will sue for a full recovery."

Donovan folded his hands in front of him and shook his head. "Sadly, Your Honor, this is not the first time the police and the District Attorney have violated my client's rights. I fear the time has come for legal action. We have every intention of filing a lawsuit for malicious prosecution, police abuse of power, and false arrest." He sighed dramatically. "The citizens of Chicago, the residents of Cook County, do not deserve a Police Force riddled with corruption and abuse. They have every right to expect untainted justice. The corrupt actions of a few threaten the freedom of many. We must put a stop to it."

Sullivan jumped to his feet. "Your Honor, that's slander."

Donovan shook his head. "It's not slander if it's true, my good sir." He cocked a well-tended eyebrow. "Prove me wrong."

The judge cleared her throat, and Donovan brought his

attention back to her.

His eyes swept her womanly charms. Judge Magnusen appeared particularly fetching after a night of . . . He shook his head and mentally scolded himself for such impure thoughts. Donovan executed a courtly bow. "Thank you for your time and consideration, Your Honor. I am confident that you will grant justice where justice is due."

Donovan pulled his head out from under Judge Shirley Magnusen's robe.

Shirley slumped back in her majestic maroon office chair and smiled. It was the smile of a sexually sated woman. She sighed with contentment. "My God, Donovan, that tongue of yours could play a concerto on a violin. Where did you learn to do *that*?"

Donovan absently stroked her creamy thigh. "Years of practice, my dear." He smiled and stood. "Let's move to the sofa, shall we? You are more than ready for my manly instrument, and believe me, it is more than ready for you."

Shirley giggled. She stood up and removed her robe, daintily hanging it on a coat tree. As she walked toward Donovan, she removed the pins from her light blonde bun and shook out her hair, the curls cascading around her shoulders. Then she kicked off her shoes and unzipped her dress, allowing it to drop to thc floor.

Donovan sat up straighter on the couch and smiled. "My God, woman. I love it when you dress like a dominatrix at a kink club." He studied the tight navy-blue corset with white lace and pink bows and purred, "You look simply delicious." He yanked her onto his lap and kissed her. His hands dug into her hair and he grasped it by the roots, pulling her mouth more tightly against his. His tongue dove into her mouth and coaxed hers into an erotic dance." He moaned. "You are going to be the death of me." He nibbled her neck, then moved to her ear, and bit down.

Shirley jerked away. "Dammit, Donovan, that hurt. I think you drew blood."

Donovan fought the lust that threatened to flood his mind. A taste of the judge's blood was so tempting. He tightened his lips over the incisors that threatened to emerge as fangs. He didn't dare expose his true nature to a woman such as Shirley. He lapped at her ear and groaned again. "I need to be inside you, darling, or I shall explode." He yanked at the corset and tore it from Shirley's body.

"Hey! I liked—"

"Shush, my dear. I need to get inside you. I must feel your velvety softness squeeze my manly pride." He gently pushed Shirley back on the sofa and parted her thighs. He took another lick. Then Donovan stood and removed his belt. He unzipped his pants and exposed his rigid cock.

"So beautiful," Shirley breathed, her voice reverent. "Please, please . . ."

Without a word, Donovan wrapped her legs around his waist and plunged inside her. He thrust artfully, rhythmically ramping up Shirley's arousal until she screamed his name.

Her eyes rolled up into her head and she collapsed onto the sofa, her limbs loose with no obvious strength. Slowly, Shirley smiled and opened her eyes. "Oh, Donovan," she cooed. "That cock of yours is magic, pure, unadulterated magic."

Donovan grinned. "Why, thank you, my dear. Always a pleasure to be of service."

Shirley smiled. "Of course, after last night, you conflicted yourself out of my courtroom. I didn't have time to act before your appearance this morning, but I will have to recuse myself during this, well, whatever this is. I will be forced to pass your case off to another judge."

"Of course, my dear. I would expect nothing less." He gazed at her and affectionately stroked her arm. "I would never compromise your integrity like that. We must ensure justice is secure, despite our . . . other pursuits."

Shirley's eyes narrowed. "Unless your skillful seduction last evening was planned. Did you intend to force me to recuse myself so you might find a more amenable judge?"

Donovan chuckled. "Judge Magnusen, I find you entirely delectable and utterly irresistible. If you will recall, I arrived at that *soiree'* with another woman on my arm. It was only after our eyes met and the heat between us almost scorched the carpet that I was forced to invite you out for a quick drink. I was not even aware you were the judge assigned to this matter until the schedule was posted early this morning. Motions hearings are always a crapshoot, you know that. It was simply too late to request a change of judge."

He gazed at her, his fingers playing with her silken hair. "Now that our attraction has been established, however, I think we need to plan for the long-term. I have no intention of ignoring our rather explosive chemistry."

Shirley's smile was tentative. "Explosive chemistry, yes. However, I should warn you. I don't share."

Donovan grinned. "And despite my reputation to the contrary, neither do I."

# Chapter Two: A Sneak Attack

Donovan raced down Michigan Avenue, his brain shutting out the sights, sounds, and smells that pierced his sensation-enhanced mind.

Sometimes, it sucked to be a vampire. Especially in this Century. One hundred years ago, the world was still a relatively quiet place. The streets weren't cluttered with honking cabs, noisy trucks with smoke-producing diesel engines, and people engaged in loud and mostly inane conversations. And the smells, Ye, Gods! Between the perfumes, colognes, food trucks and eateries, the dog parks, and industrial pollution, this New World stank. It was no surprise that many of his kind isolated themselves in their homes, shut away from the world and overstimulation of the senses. Some days, the smells alone were too much to bear.

Donovan's cell phone pinged. He pulled himself into a small alleyway, away from the stampede trudging back to their workplaces after lunch, and leaned back against a building to read a text. His face screwed up in confusion. The text read, *The first thing we do, let's kill all lawyers! Starting with you!*

"What the bloody hell?" he muttered. "Is this some kind of joke?" Donovan's eyes surveyed his surroundings. He gazed right, then left. It did not appear that someone had made him the focus of their attention. Everyone was scurrying about, like mice in pursuit of a big cheese. "Must be Finley," he said. "Finley is always plying me with lawyer jokes. He thinks he's funny."

Donovan shrugged. *Not funny at all.* He left the alleyway

and re-entered the mass migration on the sidewalk. He approached the crosswalk at Michigan and Superior and emitted a snort of frustration as the light changed and the crosswalk filled with cars. He was bumped hard by someone behind him. Donovan was forced to step into the street to regain his balance. A cab rushed by and narrowly missed clipping his side. Donovan jumped back onto the sidewalk.

A woman screamed, and Donovan jerked his head around, trying to see what all the fuss was about. The woman was pointing at him. Donovan frowned and turned away. *God save me from simpering females who saw the last issue of* City Magazine. Donovan had appeared on the cover after being named as one of Chicago's most eligible bachelors. Since then, he had learned that the female population was comprised of women of questionable morals and distressing behavior. He was growing weary of the attention. While his colleagues thought it a wise marketing strategy, it had brought him nothing but unwanted female attention. He had become prey.

Vampires were predators. They stalked their victims. Sometimes, they pursued them with a vengeance. That was why he had joined the legal profession. His predilections were well-suited to that particular world. Now, his role had apparently shifted, and he was not pleased.

Someone tapped Donovan on the shoulder. "Sir? Are you alright? You're bleeding. It appears someone stuck a knife into your side."

Donovan's mouth gaped and he turned toward the man who had spoken. Then he looked at where the man pointed. There was indeed a knife sticking out of his left side, and a stream of his blood was flowing onto the sidewalk. He had a very high threshold of pain. He hadn't felt the knife thrust into his side. If it wasn't so appalling, he would be embarrassed. Donovan opened his mouth to reply. Then the pain in his side exploded and his vision dulled. Slowly he slid onto the sidewalk, as if he planned to sit on the curb.

Then everything went black.

The panicked, high-pitched voice of his secretary, Molly MacMerkle, forced Donovan back to the present day. He opened his left eye and focused on Molly as she berated a woman clad in blue scrubs. Slowly, the other eye lifted and took in the entire scene playing out before him.

"And I'm telling you that you cannot go in there unless you are family," the woman argued. "You've already admitted that you're his secretary. That is *not* family."

Molly thrust her hands on her hips and scowled at the other woman. "I also told *you* I am his fiancée," she said in a blistering tone. She waved her left hand in front of the woman's eyes. "Take a look at this rock. That man in there gave it to *me*. Because he loves me and I love him and we intend to spend the rest of our lives together." Molly tossed her bright red hair over her shoulder and arched a sculpted brow. "The man in there is also one of Chicago's finest lawyers. If you don't let me in there, I guarantee he will sue your ass off."

Donovan tried not to chuckle. Molly would have made a fine actress. However, he doubted her fiancé, Joe, would appreciate her declaration of love for him. Finally, he moaned loudly and said groaned. "Molly, my love. I neeeeed you."

The woman in the scrubs turned, and her mouth fell open in surprise.

Molly's eyes narrowed and she glared at her. Then she brushed her aside and rushed into his hospital room, stopping at his bedside. In true Molly style, tears welled in her eyes and she wailed, "Oh, my sweet darling. What have they done to you?"

Donovan peered up at her. "Actually," he replied softly. "I was hoping you could tell me." He shifted uncomfortably. "What did I do to warrant a bed in this quacks' den?"

Molly whispered, "The cops say someone stuck you, with

a paring knife, of all things. Who did you piss off this time? A chef?"

Donovan frowned. "More likely an adversary or a dirty cop, though I can't think of anyone I angered enough to stab me. That's so uncivilized." He shuddered.

Molly nodded at the IV stuck into his arm. "Well, you lost a lot of blood. They're giving you a transfusion."

Donovan reached for the IV line, but Molly placed her hand on his. "Best not pull that out, boss. Humans don't take kindly to that. They might keep you in the hospital longer. As it is, we need to get you out of here before they discover you've miraculously healed."

"But it's human blood," Donovan hissed. "You know how I hate *that.* It's going to mess up my olfactory nerve for weeks." He scrunched his nose in disgust. "Humans already stink. Now their stink will be overwhelming."

Molly grinned. She was a werebear. She understood all too well about human stink. She much preferred to feast on cows or buffalo. They smelled sweet. Not like spoiling garbage. "Oh, just wear a mask. Tell everyone you caught a nasty case of the flu and don't want to infect anyone. Half the human population sports masks these days. It's become a fashion accessory." She smirked. "I'll buy you one. Consider it a get-well gift. Which would you prefer—Dracula or Wolverine?"

Donovan winced. "That's not even close to funny. I need something a little more classy. Something worthy of my standing."

Molly snorted. "You're a three-hundred-year-old vamp. You're lucky you *are* standing. Took you way too long to heal this time. I think you need a tune-up."

Donovan waved a hand at her and ignored her commentary. "Oh, just get whatever that designer is pushing. You know, that guy who makes my suits."

Molly made a face. "That dude's older than you and twice

as fussy. Don't blame me if he makes you something in a lavender hue."

"Whatever," Donovan said impatiently. "Ask him to send me a few samples." His gaze again landed on the IV. "You know, I haven't drained a human since the Spanish Flu pandemic in 1918. Their blood is just too tainted."

Molly gazed at him, her lips pursed. "That's such rubbish. Our blood would kill *them*. Besides, whatever is flowing through those tubes is purified."

"Doesn't matter. I want my plasma tablets. No self-respecting vamp drinks human blood anymore."

"Yes, siree, boss." Molly fell silent and looked over her shoulder. "Someone's coming. Smells like a cop." Her eyes rounded and she whispered dramatically. "Maybe they're coming to finish the job."

There was a knock at the door, and a middle-aged man wearing an ill-fitting brown tweed sport coat and rust-colored pants leaned in. "Hey, Trait. You decent in here? Wouldn't want to catch you bagging a nurse." The man chortled.

Molly made a face. "*Eeeewwww*. Not in front of me. Give it a rest, Bill. I don't need that visual in my head."

Detective William Roast stepped into the room. He swiped at a tuft of brown hair that fell into his eyes and chuckled. "Sorry, Moll. I heard you'd slipped past the old battle-ax out there." He smirked. "She says you're engaged to this bastard." He nodded at Donovan. "Does Joe know?"

Molly blushed. "No, and don't you dare tell him. That's trouble I don't need."

Bill nodded at Donovan. "So how are you doing, you old slacker? I understand you had a close call. You almost clocked out on the table."

Donovan shrugged. He couldn't tell a human that vamps don't die. When injured, their bodies automatically regenerated after a day or two. Sometimes they appeared weak or near death, but the reality was, their system had shut down temporarily to initiate the healing process. He just didn't heal as quickly anymore. When he was young, he would have been healed before they got him into the ambulance. The knife would have fallen out and the medics would have assumed they had picked up the wrong guy. By tomorrow, however, any sign of his wound would be gone. "I'm doing fine, Bill. I'm ready to get out of here. What the hell happened, anyway?"

Bill shook his head. "No one saw anything but a knife stuck in your side and blood pouring out onto the sidewalk. Then you collapsed and someone called an ambulance. You passed out."

Donovan moaned. "Great."

"Any idea who wants you dead?"

Molly giggled. "Every dirty cop, judge, and lawyer in Chicago, I imagine. You did run the knife for prints, right?"

Bill glared at Molly. "How many times do I have to tell you . . ."

"Children, play nice." Donovan pointed at Bill. "You did run the knife for prints, right?"

Bill nodded. "As soon as they pulled it out of your flabby side."

Donovan scowled. "And?"

"Wiped clean," Bill said. "Perp probably wore gloves. Doc said judging from the amount of blood you lost, you must have walked half a block before you collapsed. Did you even know you had been jacked?"

Donovan expelled a heavy breath. "Not until some woman screamed. There are so many people on those sidewalks these days, it's a challenge to remain upright." He shuddered. "All that pushing and shoving. I was lucky I wasn't trampled. So uncivil."

"Jesus, you didn't feel anything?" Bill stared at him.

"Someone *stabbed* you."

Donovan shook his head. "I simply wasn't paying attention," he lied. "I had gotten a disturbing text and was consumed by that. I wasn't paying much attention to anything else. Until the woman screamed." Donovan fell silent. He certainly wasn't going to explain his high threshold for pain to a human.

Bill gazed at him. "What's this about a disturbing text?"

Donovan sighed. "I thought it was a joke. It said, *The first thing we do, let's kill all the lawyers! Starting with you!"*

Bill's eyes widened. "And you ignored that? You didn't call me?"

Donovan shrugged. "I thought it was from your partner, Finley. You know how he's always poking at me about being a lawyer. Last month, he sent me a stuffed shark with bullet holes all over it."

Bill barked a short laugh. "Yeah. The guy thinks he's a laugh a minute. Unfortunately, the only one who laughs is Finley. The wife says it's a call for attention." He sobered. "Still, that message was aimed at lawyers, not just you. That's concerning. That means there could be more. Dammit. The last thing this city needs is another serial killer."

Molly glared at Bill. "And the last thing Donovan needs is a serial killer who won't be satisfied until he's dead. Whatchagonnado about that? Hey, copper?"

# CHAPTER THREE: OBSESSION

The high society matron could not believe her eyes. There was not a single mention of Donovan Trait's death in the Tribune. How could that be? His death should be big news. She had aimed for his kidney. And even she had witnessed him bleeding like a stuck pig

The woman's eyes narrowed. Dammit. She didn't even know where the ambulance had taken him. And calling all the hospitals in the area would create suspicion. How could she make sure Donovan Trait was really dead?

He had to be her first victim. She wanted to see the headline splashed across the front page—Donovan Trait is dead!

She had it all planned out. Each death alone made no sense. However, as the bodies piled up, her intentions would be made clear. All of the deaths were connected, someone just had to be smart enough to put all the pieces together.

Besides, damn lawyers ruled the world. They twisted the law and stomped on the innocent, all in a supposed pursuit of justice. Ha! Those bastards didn't know the meaning of the word. All they cared about was making money, stuffing their pockets with ill-gotten gains. Chicagoland would be thrilled as lawyer after lawyer met their demise.

It was important to clean out the shark pool and let the guppies rise to the top. She sighed. Her own little guppy had never gotten the chance. No, the sharks had nipped at him until there was nothing left. They had turned his life inside out. They had destroyed him. Now he lay in a cold grave, missing his momma. His momma missing him. It wasn't right. It wasn't fair.

That was why she had selected each victim so carefully. These men and women, all lawyers, all pillars of the community. The best of the best. They didn't rise to the top by working hard, by serving the poor and downtrodden. They had risen to the top by stomping on the backs of others, by chewing them up and spitting them out. They treated other lawyers like chum, like garbage upon which to feed. They deserved to die.

Besides, she had the diary. It detailed all the challenges her poor guppy had faced. Challenges those on the list had caused. And Trait, he had been the ultimate betrayal. He had claimed to be a mentor, a friend. But when her poor guppy, devastated by the actions of others, had reached out, Trait was unavailable. His inaction had forced her poor guppy's hand. He had resorted to the unthinkable.

The Lord said *An eye for an eye. A tooth for a tooth. A life for a life. Vengeance is mine, sayeth the Lord*—and this was all about vengeance. The Lord was smiling down on her. She just knew it. With his words, he had blessed her righteous mission.

*First, we kill all the lawyers.*

Donovan stared at the ceiling in the hospital room. How was he supposed to sleep when someone had tried to murder him? Ye Gods, the attempt had been made in plain sight. What kind of murderer did that? Humans had no idea what it would take to kill him. Stakes through the heart, silver bullets, or holy water were myths, as were many other folk tales. Only the removal and pickling of his brain would truly end his life. If his execution did not involve immersion of the brain in formaldehyde, he could heal. His body would spontaneously regenerate. His life force was so strong, it could recall any body part that had been removed. Except for a pickled brain. That was true death.

Donovan sighed. Incapacitating him long enough to commit murder was an impossibility. He was too strong. Yet, instinctively, he knew the murderer wasn't done. He would make another attempt. He had to get out of the hospital and home, behind locked doors. His wound had already healed. That could not be easily explained to a human. Best he went home. *Now.*

Donovan gazed through the doorway to his room. He could just see the guard Bill had posted. The man appeared to be sleeping. Should he wait out the night, or slip out now? He could mesmerize the hospital staff and the cop, sign the release papers, and head home. No one would remember. Hell, that was certainly better than sitting here, waiting to be attacked. In a hospital, he couldn't break his attacker's neck—not without an explanation. And if his attacker was another vamp, he didn't have the tools for a complete execution. Those were in his briefcase.

Finally, Donovan reached for his cell phone, which Molly had thoughtfully stuck under his pillow. He dialed a number and said, "I'm at West Hospital, Room five fifty-one. I need an extraction. A clean escape. And then transportation to my home, in Hyde Park."

Donovan disconnected and reached for the IV line. Slowly, he removed the tubing and wiped the insertion point clean with a sheet. He breathed on it until the blood clotted. He then sat up and shook his head. His body was not happy about the transfusion of human blood. His stomach would revolt later. He waited a few seconds to regain his balance. Then he stood and tossed the IV bag in a medical waste bin. Keeping his focus on the guard, Donovan went to the closet and removed the tracksuit and athletic shoes Molly had provided. He dressed quickly.

Donovan walked to the door of his room and exited. He tapped the napping cop on the shoulder and gazed into his eyes. "You can return to the station," he said softly. "Your services are no longer required." The cop nodded, stood, and silently walked away. The best time to mesmerize anyone was when they were drowsy. Their defenses were down, easily penetrated.

He moved to the nurse's station. The two on duty were already asleep. Donovan frowned—that was strange. He was startled when Molly leaped up from behind the counter. "Sorry, boss. I was looking for your release forms." She handed him a clipboard. "Sign these, and let's get out of here."

Donovan signed and Molly set the paperwork next to one of the sleeping nurses. She smirked. "Sorry, I'm not wheeling you out of here. You're going to have to walk."

"First, you need to cancel the extraction squad." Donovan smiled. "I know how you love those monkeys."

# Chapter Four: The Lady With The Gun

Donovan stalked toward the witness box.

His lips curled up into a wicked smile. "Tell me, Mr. Withers, how well do you know Alison MacAbee?" Donovan stepped away from the witness and turned to the jury box. He cocked an eyebrow. Juror Number Eight winked at him.

The witness visibly paled. "Why, I don't know her at all. We've barely met."

Donovan chuckled. "Which is it, Mr. Withers? Do you know her or not? If you've met, even barely, obviously you know her."

"Well, yes, but it's only a passing acquaintance. What I meant to say is I don't know her very well."

"I see." Donovan approached the witness stand again and rested his hand on the finely crafted wood railing. "You don't know her favorite drink or perhaps her favorite food?"

"Of course not."

"Hmmmmmm." Donovan studied the man and a smile crossed his face. He strode to the plaintiff's table and lifted a single sheet of paper, green in color. Donovan walked back to the witness stand and handed it to Withers. "However, you do know her well enough to pay the rent on her apartment in Lincoln Park, don't you?"

Withers shifted uncomfortably in his seat. "I don't know what you're talking about."

"Tell me, Mr. Withers, what is the name on that invoice?"

"Carl Arnold." He handed the invoice back to him. "That's not me."

Donovan held up a finger. "Except that the P.O. Box to which this invoice was sent *is* registered to you. In fact, we have video footage of you visiting that box and picking up your mail." Donovan grinned. "Would you like to see it?"

Withers stared at his hands and sighed. Softly, he said, "No."

"Tell me, how long have you been Alison's *Pookie Bear*?"

"Objection!" The defense attorney jumped to his feet, his eyes narrowed. "Facts not in evidence. In her testimony, Miss MacAbee never referred to anyone as *Pookie Bear*. We have no knowledge of anyone going by the name of *Pookie Bear*. The defense is fabricating evidence, as usual."

"Your Honor, I beg your indulgence. I will prove the relevance of my question."

The judge nodded. She gazed at opposing counsel. "Overruled."

Donovan stalked to the plaintiff's table and picked up another sheet of paper. He handed it to Withers. "Mr. Withers, can you please read this letter to the court?"

Withers took the paper and stared at it. He frowned, and his forehead grew shiny. He gazed at Donovan and asked, "You really want me to read this . . ."

Donovan tapped his chin. "Perhaps we can dispense with the reading of the entire letter, if you would answer two questions. Is that letter addressed to you?"

Withers flushed. "Well, yes."

"Please read the salutation."

Withers cleared his throat. "My darling Pookie Bear . . ."

Donovan danced away from the witness stand and faced the jury. "So, you *are* Pookie Bear, then?"

Withers flushed. "That's just what Alison calls me . . ."

Donovan whipped around and arched an eyebrow.

"Sounds to me like she's more than a passing acquaintance."

The defense attorney shouted, "Objection, Your Honor. There's not even a question in there." The man glared at Donovan.

Judge Hillary Lord scowled at the attorney. "And there's not a proper objection in your statement, Counselor. Either reframe the objection or zip it." She ran a finger along her bright pink lips as if zipping them.

The defense attorney shook his head and muttered, "Never mind."

Judge Lord pointed an elegantly-painted fingernail at Donovan. "And you, young man, watch your tongue. You're dancing all over the boundaries of civil procedure. I will not have you turning my courtroom into a circus." She sighed dramatically. "Since Attorney Jackson lacks the inclination to object, I will. To preserve the decorum of this court. Either frame your comment as a question or withdraw it."

Donovan smiled sweetly at the judge. "Of course, Your Honor. My humble apologies."

Several members of the jury snickered. Judge Lord banged her gavel and barked. "Does the jury wish to be cited for contempt?" She shot a stink eye at Juror Number Ten. "I imagine some of you might enjoy the accommodations at a Cook County jail. The food sucks, the inmates stink, and the guards . . ." Her face lit up with an evil grin. "Well, let's just say they were trained by a sadistic dominatrix who has a fondness for glass canes."

Several members of the jury shifted uncomfortably in their seats. Juror Number Eleven, an elderly woman in a nineteen-fifties' house dress covered by a yellow man's sweater, poked Juror Number Ten. She frowned, then made the same zipping motion.

The judge pointed her gavel at Donovan. "Attorney Trait. Do you have any further questions for this witness?"

Donovan nodded. "Just one, Your Honor." He turned to the witness. "Mr. Withers. I am a bit confused." He waved his hand and shrugged. "It happens, sometimes." The jury chuckled. "Can you please explain why you pay Ms. MacAbee's rent if you don't, in fact, know her?"

Withers buried his head in his hands and emitted a sob. He sat up straight and a single tear dripped down his face. "Okay. I do know her. I even loved her, once. But she's been threatening to go to my Emma and tell her about our affair. I just couldn't permit that to happen. So I broke things off with her and I stopped paying her rent." A bitter smile consumed his face. "If she wasn't putting out anymore, why would I continue to pay her rent?" He turned to the judge. "It's not like I promised her marriage. She was always going to be a sidepiece. She knew that. She has no right to sue for support. This lawsuit is a complete fraud. It's frivolous!"

In the gallery, a woman dressed in an elegant Chanel-like suit stood up and with a loud *harrumph* stomped out of the courtroom.

Withers ran a hand across his sweaty brow. In a voice that conceded defeat, he said, "Besides, now I'm going to need the money for a good divorce attorney."

Donovan Trait massaged the ball of Judge Marilyn Anderson's foot. He chuckled when she moaned with satisfaction.

"So nice to see you smile, my dear. You seem overly stressed." He raised an eyebrow. "In court this morning, I thought you were going to take that young lawyer out to the woodshed and spank his firm but manly ass."

Marilyn rolled her eyes. "You're the ass, brother." She snickered. "I hear you made some man cry in Judge Lord's courtroom."

Donovan's eyes narrowed. "After what he put my client through, he deserved it."

"Don't you ever get bored with winning? I mean after three hundred years, you've tried and won almost every type of case there is. Where's the thrill of victory? My word, you've never even experienced the agony of defeat. Maybe it's time to quit lawyering and move on to something else." Marilyn grinned. "Live a little."

Donovan scowled. "And why would I want to do that?

Her face became troubled. "Because I keep hearing stories about you going all Clark Gable in the courtroom. You're getting too arrogant. Some judges are itching to bury you in sanctions and let you sit in a cell for a while. Ogilvy hates you. He wants you disbarred. Prithers wants to jam his gavel where the sun don't shine. Calls you the bastard from hell." She giggled. "If he only knew." She arched an eyebrow. "And Meriweather? What the heck did you do to her? She breaks out in hives by the mere mention of your name."

Donovan smirked. "Well, there was an incident. She backed me into a corner and tried to grope my magnificent package at a Bar Association meeting. She was rather tipsy, and you know I never take advantage of women when they've over-imbibed."

Marilyn snorted. "No, you take advantage of them when they're mesmerized. Geesh, Donovan. You are very good at stepping in it. Perhaps you should stick to our kind. Besides, you know how the Coalition feels about human fraternization. Too many of those fools believe everything they read about vampires in those romance novels. If some female human finds out you're a vamp, things will go to hell, fast."

Donovan waved her off. "Never happen. Besides, I am thinking of settling down. All that carousing is losing its appeal."

"What?" The shock in Marilyn's eyes was apparent. She sat up. "Who is it? Do I know her? Vamp or human?"

Donovan smiled. "It's too early for a public announcement.

You'll just have to wait, like the rest of the family. Now back to your *judgy* friends. Think any of them hate me enough to kill me?"

His sister glared at him. "Don't change the subject," she snapped. "Who is she?"

Donovan glared right back. They had been playing this game since they were children. For some reason, Marilyn still thought she could out-stare him and force him to reveal his secrets. She had never succeeded. He held her gaze until, finally, she blinked. Donovan chortled and she smacked him in the arm. "Sooooo, any bloodthirsty enemies among the judicial troops?"

Marilyn rolled her eyes. "Those twats?" She chuckled. "Not likely. And since no attempt was made to snatch your brain, it wasn't a vamp."

"Well then, who could it be?"

"Human and female." Marilyn reached out and affectionately tugged at his hair. "Judge Shirley Magnusen, for example? I understand she is quite smitten. You are the typical romance hero, you know. Tall, dark, and handsome. You've got Dad's ice-blue eyes, Mom's aristocratic nose, and Grandpa's thick black hair. Women can't resist you. Think of the beautiful babies you and Miss Shirley could produce." She laughed. "You'd better hope the Coalition doesn't order you into their breeding program."

Donovan hid his discomfort. The last thing he needed was her interference in his relationship with Shirley. She *would* find a way to bring it to the attention of the Coalition. "Bite your tongue." Donovan snapped. "That program is abominable. I refuse to inflict that misery on a human. Get a human female pregnant and abscond with the baby at birth? We are better off contracting with a surrogate. Same result, less fuss."

"Which is why female vamps are lobbying to block it, for now. We believe there are better possibilities out there. Ones with fewer physical and emotional side effects. Besides, you know if they impregnate a human female, they need to find a way to build a stronger wall around the amniotic sac. In the past, humans miscarried when the fetus bit through the sac wall."

Donovan scowled. "That's a myth, and you know it. A fetus has no teeth. They can't bite."

Marilyn shook her head. "Vamps, even half vamps, do. Eventually, the teeth dissolve in the amniotic fluid, but until they do, a human mother is in real danger. You weren't taught that in biology because when you went to school, vamps didn't mate with humans."

Donovan shuddered. "Well, I'll leave the birthing particulars to you, Miss Marilyn," he drawled in his best southern accent. "Lordy, I don't need to be birthing no babies."

Marilyn grinned. "There's a reason the woman carries the child. A man would be bitching and complaining the whole nine months. Male vamps are no exception. Who wants to put up with *that*?" Marilyn gracefully extended her foot and examined it. She tilted her head and smiled at Donovan. "I don't suppose I could convince you to give me a pedicure?"

Donovan smiled seductively at Shirley Magnusen. "You like?" he asked gently as he trailed a finger up her naked thigh.

Shirley's gaze focused on his exposed manhood and she blushed, then she smiled contentedly. "Oh yes," she purred.

Donovan's hand grazed her stomach, then kneaded her breast. He bent down, suckled a nipple, and gently bit down. Shirley squealed, and he chuckled. "I cannot believe how sensitive you are, my darling."

Shirley's eyes rounded. "And I can't believe what you do to me. Where did you get all that stamina? First, the shower, then the kitchen, and again in my bed. I think we've suitably christened my new home." She giggled. "I haven't had that many orgasms in . . . well, forever. It's a good thing I sit on the job, because tomorrow I'm not sure I'm going to be able to walk."

"And the night has just begun, sweetness. When we're not ducking into your office or a janitor's closet, we have so much more time to explore." He lapped at her breast. "I want to taste every inch of you, without being disturbed. I'm not really a fan of sneaking around, behaving like we're teenagers. I much prefer an environment where we can make love like adults."

Shirley grabbed his face and pulled his lips to hers. When Donovan attempted to deepen the kiss, she gently pushed him onto his back. Shirley tossed her blonde hair over her shoulder and straddled him. With a sweet smile, she rubbed against him and said, "I think I've waited my whole life for you. Everyone else knows you as the world's sexiest bachelor, but the reality is even better than the myth. There's so much more to you than *this.*" Shirley swept her hand down his body. "You're smart, you're kind, you're just so giving. I hate that others can't see you as I do. Every time I see one of those posters of you in someone's office, I just want to scream at them. I hate when they see you as an object and not as a man. You deserve so much more."

Donovan felt his insides warm, which was unusual—a vampire's internal temperature usually rested at around eighty degrees. There was just something about this woman that held his attention like no other. She was a true lady, and she didn't protest when he treated her like one. Over the years, he had grown leery of opening doors and pulling out chairs because so many women took offense. Yet she simply smiled when he helped her into her coat or opened a door, allowing her to proceed before him. She was a judge, a shining example of someone who had cracked the glass ceiling, yet it had not diminished her femininity one bit.

Shirley Magnusen was all woman, and she didn't hide it.

Donovan smiled. "You humble me, darling. However, I do like how you see me, even if it's a bit embellished. Still, my qualities are far surpassed by yours. You are my angel, my heart. Other men fear you. I simply adore you."

Shirley's eyebrow rose. "Is that because of my skills in the courtroom?" She gently grasped his cock. "Or in the bedroom?" She began to stroke him.

Donovan moaned. "All of the above, and more."

Shirley rose to her knees and positioned her center over his hardness. "Show me, Donovan. Show me."

Donovan waved down a cab and jumped into the back seat. "The Criminal Courts Building, on South California Avenue, please."

The driver nodded and pulled away from the curb.

Donovan's gaze wandered to the driver. The man's light brown hair was pulled into a ponytail that ran down his back. A brown plaid flat cap was pulled low onto his face. The man's eyes repeatedly darted to the rearview mirror, as if he was nervous. Donovan studied him. He appeared to be of average height, on the thin side. The driver opened a window and the scent of jasmine wafted past Donovan's nose.

Donovan sat up straighter. *Wait a minute, that's a woman's scent. Is this a man given to feminine delights, or is it a woman pretending to be a man?* Donovan frowned. Of course, there could be all sorts of reasons for that. Maybe the person was in the middle of a gender transition. Maybe she had a fetish for men's clothing. Or maybe she was in disguise. Donovan had thought he was safe in a cab, but now he wasn't so sure.

He took out his phone and searched for Bill's number. When he found it, he initiated a call. The phone rang. After a moment, Bill picked up.

"Yeah?" he growled. "I'm about to head into the

courtroom. Gotta testify against some lug head who was groping women on the El. Whatta you want, you old shyster?"

"Oh, so you're already there? At the Criminal Courts Building? Do me a favor, meet me on the steps, please. I have a lead in that case we discussed."

The driver's eyes darted back to the mirror and gazed at Donovan. Ah, he had his or her attention now.

"I don't have time for this," Bill protested. "Didn't you hear me? I gotta testify in a few minutes."

"Oh, really?" Donovan kept his voice calm. "You found a fingerprint on the knife? Did you run the prints yet?" He forced a chuckle. "I can't wait to find out who was dumb enough to . . ."

Bill was silent. "Donovan? Are you in some sort of trouble? Do you need help?"

"Not sure, my man. Maybe. Just a little suspicious. I mean, what bonafide criminal doesn't wear gloves? Ye Gods, he could have worn mittens and the knife would be clean. What the hell was he wearing, those fishnet opera gloves or something?"

"Got it. You need help. Where are you?"

Donovan gazed out the window. "I'm on California, a few blocks away from the courthouse." His eyes moved to the taxi license. "We just passed Four Seven Eight Three Nine. We're waiting for the light to turn."

"Shit, I'm guessing that's the number on the license. Hold on, I'm calling it in now."

"Roger that," Donovan said. He breathed out a long breath as the light turned and the cab moved forward. Maybe the driver was on the up and up. Maybe he, himself, was getting paranoid. After all, he'd been out of the hospital for a week and no further attempts had been made on his life.

The cab pulled up to the criminal courts building with a

jarring stop. Without disconnecting his phone, Donovan shoved it into an inside pocket, then hastily ran his credit card through the reader and added a tip. He threw open the door and leaped from the vehicle. He wasn't waiting around for a receipt. Donovan raced up the steps and upon reaching the entrance, turned.

The cab idled at the curb as if waiting for another passenger. Not unusual in the Windy City. A suit-clad man with a briefcase walked past him, purposefully making his way toward the same cab. When he got to the vehicle, the man pulled open the door and peered in. Donovan heard him ask, "You free?" The cab driver must have responded in the negative because the man withdrew from the car and shrugged. Then he walked around the cab, apparently intent on flagging down another.

Donovan turned and entered the building.

Bill met him at the security booth. "Hey!" he shouted from the other side. "You're alive."

Donovan nodded. He placed his briefcase, keys, change, and phone on the moving belt and stepped through the scanner. As he collected his things and stuffed his possessions in his pockets, he said, "False alarm, I guess. I think I'm getting a little paranoid."

Bill slapped him on the shoulder. He took out his phone, pushed a few buttons, and held it out to Donovan. "This the guy?"

A man with unruly dark hair and a mustache stared at Donovan. He blinked. "Not even close. My driver was slight with light brown hair, no facial hair, and smelled like jasmine."

Bill gestured to his phone. "Well, this guy went off shift five hours ago. He should be home in bed. And the guy that shares his cab called in sick. The dispatcher thought the cab was in the yard. He's checking now."

"Far be it from me to make a mountain out of a molehill, but doesn't that strike you as strange?"

Bill nodded. "Sure, but that doesn't really mean anything. Cabbies switch off their vehicles all the time, especially when the guy before them had a puker. No one wants to get in a cab after that, especially if the guy before them did a shit job of cleaning up. Takes a good airing out before anyone wants to ride in it again." Bill's eyes narrowed. "You're thinking it was the same guy who knifed you?"

"Or woman. He *or she* was nervous as a cat. I was really afraid they were going to pounce. The way they kept staring at me in the rearview mirror was unnerving."

Bill laughed. "Probably saw you on the cover of some magazine. Trying to place you or something. It's not like you hide your light under a bushel. Top bachelor. Top lawyer. What's next? Most handsome?"

Donovan grinned. "If the shoe fits . . ."

Bill rolled his eyes. "Or biggest ego. Seriously, you're so visible you make my eyes hurt. The only way to protect you is house arrest. And since you've already rejected that, *and* police protection, all you can do is keep your eyes open and hope you spot any threats."

Donovan hefted his briefcase. "Last time I had police protection, you sent me someone wet behind the ears. I just knew if a gun was pointed at me, he'd squeal like a little piglet and I'd wind up protecting *him*. If I feel the need for protection, I'll hire my own." *Like a big old werewolf who's not afraid to leave an attacker without limbs.* Contrary to human myth, weres and vamps were quite friendly, thanks to an alliance they entered into in the last century. All the intermarrying had made it necessary. When a vamp married a were, they married their whole family, and while you can't pick your in-laws, you didn't want them going for your throat at every opportunity, either. In the interest of marital harmony, the Coalition had agreed to lift the ban on intermarriage among non-humans. Other creatures of the night did as well.

"Well, remember, we offered," Bill said. He checked his phone. "And I'll let you know what we find out. Now, I need to put a commuter molester away." He hurried away.

Donovan gazed at the old clock in the lobby. Just enough time to sort himself out before his trial began. Today, they were selecting jurors, and he needed to turn on the charm. He couldn't do that if his clothing was askew. He strode confidently to the nearby restrooms, chuckling at the recent addition of a unisex facility. Didn't the fools know that was an invitation for a tryst? Absently, he wondered how many lawyers, judges, bailiffs, secretaries, and law clerks had taken advantage. That wasn't his thing. The smells in a latrine did not mix well with romance.

Donovan entered the men's and straightened his tie, adjusted his suit coat, and snapped the pleats in his slacks. He brushed some hair off of his forehead. Then something flashed in the mirror and he muttered, "Oh, damn."

He watched a slim, middle-aged woman exit a stall. She was dressed as a proper matron, in a finely tailored suit. Her blonde hair was pulled back in a bun. Her face tastefully made up. The diamonds on her lobes sparkled. She was carrying a large designer-quality leather bag and held it close to her body.

Donovan spun around and grimaced. "Oh, dear, did I wander into the ladies in error?"

The woman smiled. She slowly lifted her arm and pointed it at him.

Donovan barely had time to register that she was holding a gun. He heard a click and a whispered, "Bang, bang."

He caught a light whiff of jasmine. Then everything went black.

# CHAPTER FIVE: EN FLAGRANTE DELICTO

Donovan awoke to the histrionics of his secretary. Molly. Ye God's, the woman gave Shakespeare a run for his money.

He opened his eyes and turned to her. "What are you carping . . ." He stopped and looked around. He was in his own bedroom. "How did I get . . ."

His sister, Marilyn, stepped forward. "You're lucky I have the hearing of an elephant or . . ." she smirked, "A bat. I was walking through the security checkpoint and heard you gasp. I ran toward you. Everyone thought I was hurrying toward the ladies. I found you lying on the floor in the men's bathroom. The bullet had already popped out, but blood was really flowing, so I enacted emergency measures."

"Tell me you didn't call *Mother.*"

Marilyn waved him off. "Oh, please. That would have been a disaster. I called the extraction squad. They cast an invisibility spell and got you the hell out of there."

Donovan moaned. "You called in the winged monkeys? When I was unconscious? God, they're such nosy apes. And they're thieves. Did you make sure they didn't pinch anything before they left? Last time, they sped off with half of the cow I keep in my meat locker."

Marilyn sniffed. "I still can't believe you deign to eat cow. That stuff is disgusting. Speaking of which, you're lucky I got you out of there before someone plied you with human blood, again. Last time, it took days before that got out of your system." She held her nose. "I could barely stand to be around you."

Donovan cocked an eyebrow. "Much like the scent you put off when you decided to take a bite out of mother's cat? All the *parfum* in France couldn't have rectified *that.*" His eyes narrowed. "Now what the hell happened? The last thing I remember, some woman was aiming a gun at me." A drop of blood dripped down his nose and Donovan swiped at it. "And shot me."

Molly leaned in and wiped his face with one of his fine linen handkerchiefs. He bit his lip to avoid chastising her. He could well afford to buy more, but once blood touched the linen, the scent remained, no matter how many times it was dipped in bleach. The blood and bleach combination made him gag. Donovan smiled at Molly. "Thanks, Moll. Sorry I upset you, but you know I won't die, whatever they throw at me."

Molly shrugged. "Oh, I wasn't worried about that. Queen bitch over there was getting all over my ass about not hiring you a bodyguard. Said it was my job to make sure you were adequately protected. I told her you had refused, but she . . ."

His sister glared at Molly. "Well, we'll discuss *that* later." She impatiently tapped the toe of her high-priced stiletto. "Back to the real issue. Who shot you? One of your *les amoureux*? A bitter woman you cast aside for other more lucrative delights?" An evil grin crossed her face. "It wasn't Judge Magnusen, was it?"

Donovan shook his head and frowned. "Didn't recognize this one. Besides, when I end it and they protest, I wipe their memories clean. It's less complicated that way. This one was dressed as a high society matron." He wrinkled his nose. "Very well preserved. A little too much Botox in the lips and brow. And a little too thin. Not really my type. You know I'm not into cougars. I much prefer fresher . . . uh, meat."

Molly slapped his shoulder. "That's so nineteenth century.

I keep telling you. Men don't talk about women like that anymore. You're *objectifying* human women, and some just might put a bullet in you for *that*."

Marilyn waved her off. "Even in the eighteen hundreds, he was a pig. For some reason, humans think it's cute. He gets way too many passes because he looks like some sort of movie star. Personally, I never understood why women drool over him."

"Enough!" Donovan roared. "This isn't about my failings as a man. Someone tried to kill me. *Again*. I want to know who and why." He touched the wound between his eyebrows and glared at his sister. "Did you at least save the bullet?"

Marilyn huffed. "Of course, I did." She pulled a plastic bag from her purse and held it up. "The woman who shot you used a peashooter. One of those thirty-two automatics that women carry in their purse." She chuckled. "Thing barely made a dent. Bullet popped right out."

Donovan emitted a snort. "At least that confirms she was a woman. No self-respecting man would be caught with a thirty-two. Still, if I had been human, I would probably be dead. She was certainly standing close enough. Crept right up behind me." He frowned. "I'm not going to be able to call the cops in on this. Not when the wound is practically healed. If I was human, you'd be weeping and planning my funeral."

Marilyn snickered. "Don't kid yourself. That's a recurring fantasy of mine. I plan your funeral all the time." She leaned in and yanked at his foot, still encased in a designer loafer. "Especially because you behave like a common oaf with women."

"Owww." Donovan moaned, pulling his foot out of her hand. "That hurt. Have you no decency, woman? I've been shot. I deserve a little respect." He turned to Molly. "I was supposed to be in court this morning."

Molly pursed her lips. "Do you think I'm new at this? I

called the court and told them you had taken ill. Sent that associate, Hennessey, in your place."

"*For jury selection*?"

She cast him a stink-eye. "Yes, and I went with him. You wound up with two weres and ten humans. I know the weres. They're both bears. They'll manage the others just fine." She huffed. "Did you think I'd drop the ball in your time of need?"

Donovan smiled slightly. "Thanks, and no, I knew you'd do what you had to do." He groaned. "I guess we're going to need a little help on this. Can you call that were-friend of Joe's? The one who runs that PI agency? You, know Kitty & Dumb . . ."

"It's Lynx & Dunn, boss," Molly snapped. "And I wouldn't be making fun of him if you want his help. Weres are already sensitive about the superiority complex you vamps have. Just because we sprout hair on occasion doesn't make us inferior beings. It makes us somewhat superior. All you can do is produce fangs. Heck, you can't even transform into a bat anymore." She smirked. "Evolution's a bitch, isn't it? You don't use it, you lose it. At least I can keep myself warm in the coldest of winters and, in Chicago, that's important."

Donovan emitted a long sigh. "Sorry, I'm a little moody. I don't like being shot at, even if there is no lasting damage. Anyhow, please give your friend a call. I need him to run tests on the bullet, see if he can find anything that will help me find this woman. And I'll give Bill a call and report the attempt, but I'm not going to turn over the bullet. It would be too hard to explain how I survived two wounds deadly to humans. However, I do not appreciate being dallied with. This has got to stop."

Marilyn pulled several pairs of handcuffs from her purse. "In the meantime, brother. You're under house arrest. You are not leaving your home until we find this woman. You are supposed to be dead. You need to act like it." She dangled the cuffs, her eyebrows raised. "Do I have to use these?"

"Please. Like those could hold me."

Marilyn's mouth curled slightly. "Then maybe I should just find a three-hundred-pound werewolf to sit on you. That would be most amusing."

Molly snickered. "The stench alone would keep most away. Those wolves don't bathe often enough."

Donovan rolled his eyes. "I fully intend to lay low until this matter is resolved. I'll ask Bill to contact the newspapers and report that I am in a coma and not expected to survive. That should buy me some time."

Marilyn tittered. "Thank God you wiped all those women's memories. I don't think I could survive hundreds of women wailing, bemoaning your demise."

Donovan grinned. "Hundreds? My dear sister, you wound me. Try thousands."

Bill was wearing a path in Donovan's luxurious white carpet as he paced.

Donovan was tempted to lift the stout man and plant him in a chair. "Bill, would you please sit? You're giving me whiplash."

Bill stopped and glared at Donovan. Then he huffed and sat down. Almost immediately, he jumped to his feet and moved to another. "Don't know why you buy all these antiques," he grumbled. "Not a one is comfortable. A man can't think." He pointed at Donovan. "Are you absolutely sure this isn't some woman you did the mattress mambo with? You've never seen her before?"

Donovan slowly shook his head. "Not even a shred of recognition. Nothing about her was familiar."

"What about the phony cab driver you reported? The woman who looked like a man?"

Donovan again shook his head. "One was blonde, the other

more brunette. Same color eyes, but that's it."

"Could one of them have been wearing a wig?"

Donovan frowned. "A disguise? How would I know that unless we got into a tussle and I knocked it off?"

"What about the scent? You said the cab driver smelled like jasmine. What about the other? Was the scent the same?"

Donovan cocked his head. "I'm not in the habit of sniffing females, Bill, especially when they're pointing a gun at me. I save the sniffing for when we're *in flagrante delicto.*"

Bill stared at him. "In flagrante what? Just use the word, man. You only smell woman you fuck."

Donovan shuddered. "That word is just so *gauche,* Bill. At least say *made love to* or *slept with.* It's much more refined."

Bill snorted. "When a chick tries to off you, there's no time to be refined. Now focus. The scent? Anything else I can use to find the perp?"

A frustrated expression crossed Donovan's face. "The scent. I had a fleeting sense of jasmine, but I don't know. When someone points a gun at you, you're not thinking, *they smell of jasmine,* you're thinking, *they're going to shoot me.*" He threw up his hands. "I already showed you the text on my phone. It has to be the same person. Other than that, I can't think of a thing. I can't even think of anything I have done that would warrant a bullet. Sure, the D.A. and certain prosecutors resent me. I tend to leave them weeping in their mother's milk. But that's because I'm a good lawyer. I'm not a trickster or a shyster. I'm just good at my job. You don't kill a lawyer for that."

*"Weeping in their mother's milk?* Geesh, sometimes you sound like you're from another century. Like one of those movies with those lords and ladies my wife is so fond of. That Darcy fella. Sometimes, you sound just like him."

Donovan tried to smile. Really, he did. Unfortunately, that remark hit a little too close to home. Jane Austen's characters in *Pride and Prejudice* were not unfamiliar to him. They could have been his cohorts at one time. His childhood friends. The true bloods. Those born to vampire parents when that was still possible. Those blokes had accompanied him to Eton and Oxford. It had been a time of innocence and secrets. A coming of age. Fighting not only hormones, but the onset of a deadly thirst for blood. How many humans had he cast aside after bloodlust overcame him and he was forced to satisfy his thirst or die?

He had begged and begged his father, a chemist, to find a solution. First, it was plasma harvested from people bound for Potter's Field. That was kept in an apothecary bottle. Then his father had developed powdered blood that could be carried in a pouch and mixed with red wine. In the twentieth century, the powder was contained within a tiny capsule and taken by the mouth, not unlike a vitamin. His father had carefully crafted this compound, adding a little-known spice to make the pill unpalatable to humans.

Since that formulary, his father had branched off into seasonings and spices that could be used on traditional human foods. His parents were now developing an entire line of frozen meals, home-delivered to the discerning vamp.

These developments had made it much easier for vampires to integrate into the human world and, in fact, had altered their metabolism so that sunlight no longer burned their retinas, rendering them blind. Sunglasses were still required for prolonged exposure, but most vamps were now able to survive limited exposure to natural light.

The only thing chemists had been unable to resolve was the garlic problem. It still didn't repel vampires—that was a myth put forth by garlic farmers to increase sales—but when it was cooked, the stink was so all-consuming, vampires were left gasping for air. That was why so many avoided French or Italian cuisine. The reliance on garlic was simply not tolerable.

When a popular chef on one of those cooking shows suggested that a sweet onion was more akin to the wild garlic of old and provided better flavor, the man found his empire expanding exponentially, due to heavy investment by vamps.

Of course, garlic jokes were quite prevalent among his peers.

*Why do vampires prefer strippers who wear garlic? Because they lose their cloves.*

Barely funny, but worth an amused groan. Donovan sighed. "Be that as it may, Bill, it has been suggested that I die and remain dead, euphemistically, of course."

Bill stroked his chin. "I suppose we could leak something to the press. Put it on the Internet. Maybe lure the perp out. Force her to make another attempt." He smirked. "*The lawyer who wouldn't die.* That might make a good movie."

Donovan scowled. "For now, let's suggest I am on my death bed. Maybe monitor calls to the hospital, see who's interested in my demise."

Bill shook his head. "Naw, I want it better contained. Hospitals leak worse than my toilet. Someone always talks. Could blow the whole sting. Let's just say you've been moved to an undisclosed location to ensure privacy in your final days. Then people will have to call your secretary to inquire."

"They'll just assume I am at home. The last thing I want is someone breaking in here and coming after me in my sleep."

Bill gazed around the room. "This place is a fortress. You've got every door and window wired. You even have generator backup if you lose power. Unless someone gets to the generator, which is in your basement, they can't get to you."

"Where there's a will, there's a way. This woman seems motivated. Let's just say I'm in hospice care at a private facility. However, I am going to hire round-the-clock protection for Molly. I don't want her to be accosted by the media or the perp as they try to ferret out my location. She doesn't deserve that." He smiled. "And they'll also be all over you, too, demanding answers."

Bill shrugged. "Comes with the territory." He stood and stretched, his shirt popping out of his pants. "Meanwhile, I'll get Moll's coms set up so we can track inquiries." He adjusted his clothing, then pointed at Donovan. "You need to stay put. You can prance down Michigan Avenue, pretending you've risen from the dead, when this is over. Take one of those staycations the wife is always talking about. Nap. Eat bonbons. Binge-watch one of those Zombie shows."

Donovan groaned. He gazed at Bill. "I'll be good. And you. At least pretend you're upset that one of your Poker buddies is near death."

Bill tapped his chin. "Let's see. The guy who cheats at Poker and always cleans my clock is near death? I'm going to be celebrating." He laughed. "Nope, not going to be upset at all."

# Chapter Six: Death Becomes You

The elegantly dressed woman glared at The Tribune. *The bastard is near death, and all he gets is a story on page three?* Maybe Donovan Trait isn't as well-respected as she had thought. She frowned, wrinkles marring her forehead. *Or maybe they are just waiting until he died. Then his death would make Page One.*

She sighed and read the news story again:

*Prominent Chicago Attorney Donovan J. Trait was shot by an unknown assailant Friday. Police say he is now fighting for his life at an undisclosed location.*

*According to a statement issued by the Chicago Police Department, Trait was found unconscious with a gunshot wound to the head Friday morning at the Criminal Courts Building. Self-harm has been ruled out. Tests for gunshot residue on Trait's hands were negative, according to Police Det. William Roast. "It is clear that an attempt was made on Mr. Trait's life and an investigation is ongoing,"*

*Roast also said he is currently interviewing people of interest. Meanwhile, he said, Trait is receiving medical care at an undisclosed location. "Sadly, doctors hold little hope for his recovery," Roast said.*

*Trait's law office issued the following statement: "Our thoughts and prayers are with our colleague, Donovan Trait, who was cruelly struck down while pursuing justice for a client. We have been told by doctors that after surgery, Attorney Trait remains in a coma and is in critical condition. Apparently, there is minimal brain activity, and if Attorney Trait does survive, doctors say he may not emerge from a vegetative state. We are devastated by this news. He will be missed."*

*Trait has led an illustrious legal career, winning significant victories for his clients. He has received numerous awards for his pro bono work with the homeless and the underprivileged. However, Trait is most known for his dashing good looks. He has been named Chicago Bachelor of the Year, Chicago Hottie of the Law, and the Lawyer Chicago Women Fantasize About, a nod to his good looks and engaging personality.*

The socialite frowned. The police had not disclosed the message she had sent to Trait. Did they even find it? She didn't want people to think he was killed by some worthless slut who pined for his body. She needed them to know why he died. That he was a symbol of a warped justice system. That he had subverted the law for his own ends. That he was one of the lawyers responsible for her little guppy's death.

She set the paper next to her cup of tea and toyed with the silver spoon that sat next to a saucer. Perhaps it was time to pen a note to the Tribune to make it clear why Donovan Trait had to die.

*No, patience.* That would be more appropriate after he died. Then no one would mourn his death. He would be scorned as he spent the rest of his days in the cold hard ground.

Just like her dear little guppy.

The woman sighed. It was time to move on. Donovan Trait was as good as dead. Her next victim would be much easier to kill. Hell, she doubted this one would even be mourned.

She giggled. She was quite sure the rotund man had never been named Chicago Hottie of the Year. Disgust filled her. She would be surprised if this one could find his own dick.

She tapped the tip of her saucer with a finely manicured nail. Now, how should she kill this one? There were so many ways. A car accident? A fall? Poison? Oh, maybe a pillow held down over his face. No, that would give him a chance to fight back. She needed something quick and final. She took a sip of her tea.

He was a glutton. Clearly, he should die a glutton's death.

Donovan tossed the final newspaper onto the floor next to his bed. Ye Gods, you'd think all his legal accomplishments had meant nothing. He had slain the dragons of industry and righted wrongs inflicted on the less fortunate, but no one seemed to care. All they could talk about was the fact that women and some men found him attractive. That was almost insulting.

He sighed. Donovan was long past stuffing his pockets with cash. He had made his millions a century ago. He didn't need any more money. As far as he was concerned, America's greatest shame was the fact that it failed to aid people who were hungry and homeless. It grated at him every time he passed someone dressed in rags, huddled in a doorstep, or a woman with a passel of children begging on the street. Where had the humanity in the human world gone?

He frowned. Throughout his life, he had always tried to aid the poor. Arranging for meals to be provided to the hungry, a little coin slipped to the unemployed. Through the centuries, governments had done little to aid those in need, and when they did, it was in ways that marginalized them. He had been appalled by the workhouses in the nineteenth century. Those places had been hell holes. The conditions much like the sweatshops of the twentieth century.

Donovan ran a hand through his hair. Not much had changed. There would always be people who took advantage of the poor. The poor would always be gullible, driven by desperation. All he could do was try to make a difference in his corner of the world. He no longer had the innocence of youth. He knew he couldn't save everyone on this Earth.

Still, his impending death had given him a bird's eye view of his legacy, and he found it disturbing. He would need to work harder.

His cell phone chirped. A message. Donovan picked up his phone and scrolled through the numerous texts that had popped up. It amused him that despite the fact he was supposed to be in a coma, he had been inundated with texts expressing well-wishes. It had gotten so bad he had secured a new phone to communicate with Molly, Marilyn, and Bill. They were the only ones who had his new number.

He checked his phone. Molly had sent him a text. He clicked on the appropriate icon.

"Donovan! Your *amour*, Judge Shirley, is becoming a pest. If I have to listen to her wail about losing the love of her life one more time, I swear I am going to march over to the courthouse and rip out the little twit's throat. How do I shut that yappy broad down?"

Donovan smiled. He was touched by Shirley's affection. She had proved to be a worthy companion in bed and out. If she was a vamp, he would be entirely smitten. Unfortunately, she was remarkably human and given to the overheated emotional responses of which her kind was so fond. While it bothered him to subject her to such unhappiness, he had no choice. To fool a killer, it was necessary to pull the wool over everyone's eyes.

Donovan typed back, "Her affection pleases me. It almost makes this subterfuge worth it. Give her something to do. Maybe write my eulogy?"

"Why not just tell her the truth? Put her out of her misery?"

Donovan chuckled. That would make it easier for Molly, not him. He responded, "She's a horrible actress. If my true fate was revealed, she would walk around smiling and give everything away. I can't risk that."

Molly sent him a frowning emoji.

He typed, "You do have this phone locked down and out of sight, right?"

"Of course. I'm not stupid."

"Well, buck up. This will be over soon, I hope."

A pair of praying hands appeared.

Donovan chuckled. He responded, "I doubt prayers will help. However, make sure you play your part in this drama. You are about to lose your beloved boss. You should be beside yourself."

"Unlike Shirley, I can act."

Donovan heard a commotion outside his door. He shoved the phone under his pillow just as Bill burst into the room.

That he was out of sorts was apparent. "Dammit, Donovan," he sputtered. "There was another attack. Another lawyer. This one's dead." He wrinkled his nose as if he had sniffed Limburger cheese. "That ambulance chaser. The one with all of the ads on television."

Donovan swung his legs over the side of the bed and frowned. "Charles Wilson? How the heck did someone get to him? He has more protection than the president."

Bill shrugged. "Poison, we think. He collapsed at his desk after drinking something from one of those overly priced coffee shops. Looked like a heart attack. But the coffee smelled funny and his lips had a blue tinge, so my guess is poison."

Donovan's eyes narrowed. "That's a woman's instrument of death. Men are less delicate. They prefer something more brutal. Was there a note?"

Bill shook his head. "Not at the scene, but after we checked his phone, we found the same text message that had been sent to you. *The first thing we do, let's kill all the lawyers! And you're next!*"

"So we've got a *female* serial killer targeting lawyers?"

"Maybe. Unlike you, that guy had a lot of enemies. He put the *eaze* in sleaze. Dude was not well liked. Even his clients hated him. He had quite an operation going. He only took cases that could be settled for big money. Then he took his contingency fee and billed the client for *expenses,* leaving them with almost nothing."

Donovan sniffed. "I've heard of him. He settles for far less than the cases are worth. Some of his clients have gone to colleagues, dissatisfied with the low payouts. They were so disabled they were unable to work and needed some sort of financial support for the remainder of their lives. Instead, they were left with almost nothing. Unfortunately, there wasn't much I could do for them. They effectively signed away their rights. They permitted him to settle for whatever he thought appropriate. They saw dollar signs. He wanted a quick payday.

"The man gave lawyers a bad name."

Bill sat in an armchair. "Yeah, some of the guys at the shop have used him for car accidents. They were not very happy with the results." He leaned forward and gazed at Donovan. "The thing that puzzles me, though, is the lack of connection between you and him. I mean, you're a classy guy. You actually help people. Everyone I know who has hired you has walked away happy. Old Chuckie, not so much. As far as ethics go, the difference is night and day. So why you *and* him? It makes no sense."

"Maybe different killers? For different reasons? Shakespeare's quote about lawyers is not obscure. It is oft-repeated. And unfortunately, not all lawyers are worthy of affection. Some are deserving of the disdain they receive."

Bill narrowed his eyes and tapped on his leg, considering Donovan's reply. Finally, he said, "Maybe it could be as simple as that. But I don't know. It seems to me there had to be some sort of pattern. A reason the two of you have been grouped together. A reason for the attacks."

"Well, I don't know Charles Wilson. We've never even met. At Bar Association meetings, he walks in with his entourage and holds court during the happy hour. He doesn't even attempt to socialize. But you're right. We appeal to an entirely different clientele. I don't see any connection either."

Bill stood. "Maybe it's random, but that's not how a serial killer thinks. In his or her mind, you're linked. If we figure out the connection, it will be easier to find her or him. We still don't know what we're looking at."

"If it helps, I can have Molly run a comparison of filings. See if there are any links there. We can also compare client last names, see if maybe we've represented clients from the same family."

Bill shrugged. "It's worth a try. I hope it's that easy. Otherwise, I don't have a clue where to start. They left no visible evidence behind. We tried to track the phone number for the texts, but that was a bust. They all came from different numbers, all burner phones. Right now, we suspect it may have been the same killer because of the message. And we're speculating that it's a woman. A very smart woman. Most would have used one phone.

"That sketch you gave us wasn't much help. She looks like half the women in Chicago. Nothing distinctive about her at all. Perhaps if you'd seduced her first, we would have gotten something more. A strange mole or something." Bill waved his hand, his expression one of frustration. "Anyway, let Molly work her magic. Maybe she'll come up with something." He smirked. "It's not like she doesn't have the time—with you being near death and all."

The high society matron clapped her hands with glee.

Charles Wilson was dead, and his murder had warranted a headline on the front page. The man was a skunk, but he was well-known. And he practically kept the local television stations afloat. He did so much advertising, it was annoying.

She could recite his slogan in her sleep: "No problem too big or too small. We do it all."

The schmuck hauled in the poor clients and made them repeat the stupid slogan in his ads. It was very off-putting.

Still, this kill had been easy. She had merely delivered the coffee and some pastries to his office, along with a note that said *From a grateful client.* The narcissistic fool never questioned it. He thought it was his due. He had simply stuffed his pie-hole and then collapsed, well on his way to another realm before anyone even realized he required assistance.

The woman studied her list of targets. Time to shake things up a bit. A different weapon, perhaps? She smiled. She was lucky her father had been a car mechanic. She had learned so much at his side. Why, she could turn a vehicle into a veritable killing machine. The woman took a sip of her tea. Yes, this time a car accident would suit.

Or maybe some sort of bomb. These days, you could get instructions for building explosive devices off the Internet. And those were so easy to detonate. Simply attach a cell phone and detonate from another city. Boom. Dead guy. She giggled. So many ways, so little time.

She just needed to pick an appropriate target. Someone whose departure would leave the legal community in despair. Which lawyer's demise would best avenge her poor guppy's death?

She felt the air stir about her. She forced a smile onto her face as her husband entered the room. The old fart hadn't a clue as to what she what capable of. He saw her as a trophy wife. Arm candy. Someone to entertain his friends.

How she hated getting into his bed at night. It took everything within her not to gag when she was pulled into his sagging, wrinkled arms. She wanted to shudder at the lengths to which she was forced to submit to his twisted sexual needs. Her father had been right. When you marry for money, you wind up paying for it.

She withheld a smirk. Yes, the old coot would be her last kill. That would really confuse the cops. He had nothing in common with the others, other than holding a law license. But he had done nothing to alter the chain of events that led to her poor guppy's death, so he had made her list.

She would go out like a blazing inferno. And so would he.

Donovan stared at the printout Molly had emailed him. How was it possible that he and Chuckie had no clients in common? Not even on opposing sides. Sure, Chuckie's game was insurance settlements. Donovan preferred to battle personal injury out in court. Still, somehow, Chuckie had managed to avoid even a single appearance before a judge.

Donovan's mouth curled in distaste. The man hadn't practiced law, he had pandered to the insurance companies. It wasn't the first time he had encountered such bad lawyering. Because he did not age, Donovan had been forced to move on to different jurisdictions, even different countries, throughout the centuries. He had witnessed inferior lawyering almost everywhere. Still, this guy was at the bottom of the heap.

Donovan shifted to another screen and checked out Charles Wilson's biography. His disgust grew. The man had attended law school in a state that formerly had diploma privilege. Wilson had probably skated through school with a C average and was admitted to the Bar without even passing a bar exam. Not every attorney admitted to the Bar by diploma privilege was inferior, of course. It was just that Donovan was never surprised when one was.

Donovan reread Chuckie's biography. There had to be something they had in common. Why else would a killer target both of them? Donovan paused. Court-approved settlements and court filings were a matter of public record. What if this involved a client who never filed a lawsuit? A settlement Chuckie considered a slam-dunk, so it was handled privately, without court supervision? Some companies actively worked to avoid the bad public relations associated with a lawsuit, whether that lawsuit had merit or not

He dialed Molly's private cell phone.

She connected in her usual snarky way. "A voice from the great beyond! Boss, you're supposed to be near death. You're in a coma. Whatdidyado? Bribe some horny nurse to dial for you?" She cackled. "Sometimes, it's just too easy . . ."

Donovan rolled his eyes. "Good thing your boss isn't one of those stuffy old lawyers who demand respect, Moll. You'd be in the unemployment line. Say, that's not a bad idea. You're starting to show your age. Maybe a younger WereBear is in order."

Molly fell silent. Finally, she said, "That's such a low blow, I don't see how you'll ever dig yourself out of it. Good thing I know you're kidding. Otherwise, I'd sic Joe on you. He loves the taste of a vampire. He says your kind makes a tasty meal."

Donovan tried to hide the smile in his voice. "You should never have hooked up with a WereLion, Moll. Those guys are cannibals."

Molly laughed. "Better than a bloodsucker! But I digress. To what do I owe the honor of your call?"

"Did you ever get in touch with that PI? The Lynx? The one who can hack into anything? I need a favor."

"I left a message. He never called back. I heard he was sunning on a beach in the Mediterranean. What do you need?"

"I want to know if Charles Wilson and I have ever had a client in common. Your search of public records produced nothing, so I need to break into his client records."

Molly cleared her throat. "Attorney-client privilege, Boss. That information's protected. You'd be breaking so many rules, it isn't funny. And we all know how you feel about rules."

"*Rules are meant to be broken*. That's *your* most inappropriate advice, Moll. Maybe this time, you're right. However, I have no choice. I need to know if there is some link between me and Chuckie. The police are getting nowhere. I need to figure this out."

Molly emitted a long-suffering sigh, the kind his mother excelled at. "Okay, I guess I can call The Lynx. again. But that guy ain't cheap. He lives an extravagant lifestyle. He has very expensive tastes. You're going to have to open your wallet and part with some cash."

"Whatever it takes, Moll. I spare no expense when it's my life."

Molly sniffed. "What are you worried about, Boss? You can't kill a vamp. Well, not easily. It's not like some ninety-eight-pound woman could . . ."

"But she can try, Moll. It's the repeated attempts that make me leery. If she tries again, and I don't die, I will have to leave town. The humans will demand an explanation, and I don't think they will respond favorably to the only one I have.

"I happen to like Chicago, bad winters and all. I would like to stick around for a while."

# Chapter Seven: The Lynx

Molly tapped her foot impatiently.

The Lynx cocked an eyebrow, and his brown cat eyes flashed green with greed. He picked up the fine bourbon contained in an expensive crystal glass and swirled it as if contemplating. "This time, it will cost him," he purred.

"What do you want? A million?"

"I want unlimited access to the family jet. I love to travel in style, and everyone knows the Traits spare no expense when traveling."

Molly scowled. "And how are they supposed to get the stink of cat out of the carpet?"

"I understand *Madame Trait* adores cats. Why, she has several Persians as pets." He plucked at his light brown mustache, which looked a bit like whiskers. "That should not be a problem." He gave Molly a hard stare.

Molly shrugged. "It's out of my hands. Donovan doesn't own the jet. His parents do, and he doesn't like involving his parents in his business. They are happily living their life in Tenerife. Off the coast of Spain. They don't even know he was attacked, and I'm quite sure he would not want them upset." She shook her head. "So, no deal. State your price, *in cash*." Molly narrowed her eyes. "It's a simple hack. It should take you ten minutes."

The Lynx tilted his head. "If it's so easy, why couldn't you do it, my all-knowing bear? Too complex for that Grizzly mind?" He peered at his fingernails, then cast her a sly smile.

Molly bristled. The Lynx was such an ass. "For your

information, I don't want the hack to be traced to me. And I am supposed to be in mourning. I've got to do that human weepy shit. I am on leave while my boss hangs on to life by a thread. I don't have access to what I need."

The Lynx rolled his eyes. "Whatever." He lifted his glass of bourbon to his lips and sipped. His feline tongue darted out to catch an errant drop. "One million and a bottle of that rare bourbon Donovan keeps in his cellar. It has a hint of vanilla and caramel so pleasing to the palate." He waved his hand. "I don't need all of the frou-frou packaging. Just the bottle." He emitted a sensual purr. "Just something to enjoy while I undertake such a boring task."

He gazed at her, his thin lips attempting a grin. "Final offer."

Molly frowned. Donovan guarded his bourbon like it was pure gold. He would not be pleased if she gave away his beloved liquor, especially to a skanky Lynx. "No can do on the bourbon, cat. One million even. You can buy your own bottle of booze."

The Lynx narrowed his eyes and leaned closer. He gazed into her eyes and intoned, "Look into my eyes, my dear. My wish is your command. You will submit to my—"

Molly giggled. Then, a tear slid from her eye. She bent over at the waist and let out a belly laugh. Finally, she stood and glared at The Lynx. "Do. Not. Use. That. Mesmerizing. Shit. On. Me. You. Lowlife. Horsefucker."

The Lynx reared back and stared at her. He held up his hands. "Now, now. I was merely trying to—"

Molly stabbed at his chest. "I want to take a bite out of you right now, bucko. You will not try to use your sleazy cocktail tricks on me." She pulled her purse onto her shoulder and said, "I will take my business elsewhere." She turned and stomped to The Lynx's front door.

The Lynx hissed, then scurried after her. "Hey, hey," he

said, attempting to placate her. "I was just kidding around. A million is fine. I will do the job." He swept his arm back toward his library. "Shall we discuss the details?"

Molly muttered, "This is what I get for trying to deal with a damn cat."

Donovan picked up the remote and powered the television. He could not remember ever being this bored. The large screen burst to life, apparently just in time for a special report.

A news anchor Donovan recognized announced, "An active shooter situation has developed at the law firm of Melton and Morris. We now go to our reporter, Morry Levitch, in the Chicago Loop."

A middle-aged man, dressed in a blue suit with a red tie, squinted into camera range and drawled, "Well, Debby, earlier today, the Chicago Police were called to this prominent firm after it was reported that shots had been fired. The firm has been on lockdown since. The employees have been ordered to shelter in place. About ten minutes ago, a SWAT team arrived and entered to begin an office to office sweep."

The anchor, Deborah James, asked, "Any word on who was shot?"

Morry shook his head. "No. The police have been communicating with someone within the firm, but have not shared what they learned or who they've been speaking to."

"What about the shooter? Is he still within the firm?"

Morry frowned. "Unfortunately, Debby, we don't have that information. I imagine we won't know anything until the SWAT team completes their sweep of the building."

Debby smiled and fluttered her eyelashes. "Well, while we wait, can you describe how a SWAT team works? What exactly are they doing in there? In fact, I bet some of our listeners don't even know what SWAT means." She gazed directly into the camera. "I assure you they aren't swatting criminals." She chuckled, then fell silent.

Donovan snorted. "That's what you get for putting a dumb blonde on the news desk, you idiots." He shook his head. "Debby, the dumb-dumb. That money she spent on enhancing her breasts would have been better spent on reversing her lobotomy."

Morry stared into the camera, obviously nonplussed. Finally, he said, "Well, Debby, SWAT stands for *special weapons and tactics*. These fine men and women are trained to deal with life-threatening situations. They engage in dangerous encounters with deadly criminals to save lives and diffuse hostile conflicts. SWAT teams are true American heroes."

Debby squinted into the camera. She made a sweeping motion with her arm. "And in the end, they swat the perp and put them away." She giggled again.

Morry's eyes widened and he emitted a strange sound. Kind of like laughter, but more like a scowl. There was an awkward pause, then the rescue squad located behind Morry suddenly sprang into action. The back doors to their vehicle opened, two emergency technicians jumped out, pulled a gurney from the vehicle, and ran into the building. "It looks like the EMT's are going in," he said.

"Well, they probably have a survivor," Debby replied. "If the victim was dead, the medical examiner's office would have been called. Everyone knows that."

Morry swung back toward the camera and blinked. "Well, let's not put the cart before the horse, as they say." He turned back to the building. The EMTs emerged with the gurney, which now carried a black body bag. Morry turned his head and spoke into his microphone. "Sadly, there appears to be a casualty, Debby. They don't put live victims in body bags."

Debby's red lips curled into a pout. "Any idea who it is?"

"Seeing as the victim is in a body bag, I can't identify the body, Debby." His eyes darted behind him and he said. "Wait, the police are coming back out." He ran toward one of the members of the SWAT team. Several other reporters crowded in, sticking their mics in the face of the man in the lead.

"What did you find in there?" one shouted.

"Did you get the shooter?" another asked.

Morry pushed in front of the group and queried, "Whose body was on the gurney?"

The officer slowly removed his helmet. He waved at two patrolmen and pointed to several yellow sawhorses typically used in barricades. Immediately, the men moved the horses, ran *crime scene tape* between them, effectively cutting off the entrance to the building.

The officer held up his hand and everyone fell silent. "My name is Commander Davis L. McDonald and this is my team." He gestured toward the people dressed in tactical gear behind him. "Less than an hour ago, we responded to a call that indicated there was an active shooter in the building and that people had been shot. The entire building went into lockdown. All tenants sheltered in place.

"Upon further investigation, we learned that a shooting had occurred in an elevator that led to the offices of Melton and Morris, and it was believed that the shooter was still in that part of the building. However, when my tactical team entered the premises, we could not find the perpetrator. He or she may still be in the building, so it remains on lockdown until we can do a complete sweep.

"Right now, we believe there is only one casualty. We cannot release his name until we have notified his family, but suffice to say he was a prominent Chicago attorney."

The media began to shout questions, but McDonald again held up his hand. "We will provide more information when it becomes available. Right now, I ask that you step back and let us do our job. That means do not, under any circumstances, enter the building. Anyone crossing this barricade will be detained. Anyone attempting to enter the building without authorization will be shot." He smirked. "See those guns on my officers' belts? They know how to use them. Now behave and let us do our jobs."

Morry walked away from the crowd and faced the camera. "Well, there you have it, Debby. Another prominent lawyer murdered in a matter of weeks. First, Donovan Trait. Then, Charles Wilson. Now, a third death. Coincidence or pattern? Perhaps there's a serial killer out there that has a beef with lawyers." The man could barely contain his mirth.

Debby smiled. "Well, Shakespeare did say something about killing all lawyers. Perhaps someone is taking it literally." She rolled her eyes and chuckled. "Only in Chicago."

Donovan glared at the TV. "Stupid people. I'm not dead. Check your damn facts." He scratched the side of his face and muttered, "Everyone hates lawyers until they need them to pull their arses out of the fire." He shut off the television. He knew no one from the firm of Melton and Morris, either. That was a labor and employment firm, an area of specialty in which he had no expertise at all. The killer had to be murdering lawyers at random.

That wasn't good. Not good at all.

The Lynx answered his phone and purred, "Yes, my love?"

"Oh, for cripes sake, Lynx. We are not in love. I don't even like you."

He chortled. "Give it time. Eventually, you will fall . . . for my charms. I am *irresistible*."

Molly laughed. "Yeah, keep telling yourself that, asshole."

The Lynx meowed. "Is there a reason for this call, Miss Molly? Or did you merely call to deny your attraction to me?"

He preened. "Denial isn't good for the soul, you know. But pleasure? That, my dear, should be your priority in life."

Molly sputtered, "Are you nuts? I have half a mind to come over there, bring out my bear, and sit on you."

"Ohhhhhh, Miss Molly. Will you, please? I so enjoy being topped." He shivered. "That would be such an orgasmic delight."

There was silence.

Finally, The Lynx inquired, "Miss Molly? Are you there?" He meowed again.

"I was considering the best way to kill you, you . . . you, jackal."

The Lynx emitted a sharp breath and clutched a hand to his chest. "You wound me, my pet. How dare you compare me to those wild dogs? They're worse than coyotes. So unrefined. With a lynx, you are guaranteed a modicum of class. With a jackal, you have literally gone to the dogs." He paused. "Now what can I do for you, my sweet teddy bear?"

Molly harrumphed. "I need to expand the scope of your employment."

"This time, will a fine bottle of bourbon be involved?"

Molly sighed. "My instructions are to give you that bottle only if you get results. I need you to figure out what Donovan's connection is to the Wilson firm and now, a firm called Melton and Morris."

The Lynx's eyes narrowed. "Other than clients?"

"Any and everything, cat. Employees, summer clerks, Christmas parties, favorite wines. Anything that could connect Donovan to Charles Wilson and Robert Melton. Go back five years. That's how long Donovan has practiced law in Chicago."

"Robert Melton? He was the latest attorney on the murderer's list? Oh my, my cousin, Ricardo, dated his secretary. What a small world."

The Lynx's superior hearing caught the whir of a computer in the background. "I sense I don't have your full attention, my dear. Really, doing secretarial work while conversing with me is beneath you. I am rather insulted."

"I am sending you a new contract as we speak, you idiot. Sign it and return, please."

"And the bottle of bourbon?"

"Will be provided to you upon successful completion of the contract. Not a minute before."

The Lynx meowed. "I do love a woman who drives a hard bargain, especially when she threatens to sit on me."

"Can it, cat. And get busy. This may be a matter of life or death. And cat?"

"Yes, my sweet honey bear?"

"Trim those tufts of hair in your ears. They're gross."

"I think not, my love. How else can I rejoice in your sweet dulcet tones?"

Molly snorted and disconnected the call.

# Chapter Eight: Judge Shirley

Donovan closed the paperback book he was reading and sighed.

Either Molly had a sadistic streak or she was a closet romantic. He had asked for some classics. She apparently thought a series of books about a sadistic billionaire who delighted in whipping innocent young women fulfilled his request. He laid his head against the back of the armchair in which he was sitting and groaned. Such drivel. If someone is going to write a book about BDSM, they should at least get it right.

Now, he and the sweet Judge Shirley Magnusen knew what they were doing. They had fallen into their roles naturally. Though Shirley was an alpha on the bench, her surrender in the bedroom was pleasing and sweet. He didn't need to get her drunk to gain her submission. He just gently coaxed it out of her. Maybe he should write his own torrid romance, with cuffs and blindfolds and other devices. God knew the dreck Molly was reading was simply misleading. She might require some proper guidance.

No wonder humans were so screwed up. They understood nothing about passion and romance. About the pleasures of dominance and submission. Handcuffs and blindfolds were so old school. No, a true Dominant understood how to play a submissive's body like a Stradivarius and captivate their mind. It was all about connection, an intimacy that melded the mind, heart, and soul. His adorable Miss Magnusen entrusted him with all of that. That was what true romance was.

Intimacy. Most humans just didn't get that.

Donovan conjured sweet Shirley's face in his mind. When she unleashed her tight blonde bun and those curls draped over her perfectly shaped breasts, her blue eyes lit with anticipation and her cherry red lips trembling with need, his ancient heart filled with pride, and lust, most definitely lust. It was too bad that he had long ago given up on love. No female vampire excited him. Since he was one of the few pureblood vampires left in the world, his mate must have vampire blood, even if it was a human turned rather than born.

He had considered turning Shirley, but she was so decadently human. Female vamps quashed passion for duty, but there was nothing dutiful about Shirley in the bedroom. His luscious judge was all woman, possessed with an insatiable curiosity and a willingness to please. She would try anything once. Donovan chuckled. Or twice.

He knew he had captured her adoration. The feeling was mutual. When he held her in his arms, he felt complete. Could he ask her to sacrifice her life as a judge to join his? His inability to age was not necessarily a positive. When those around you began to wrinkle and gray, and you did not, questions were inevitable. As was resentment. Many times, he had been forced to move to qualm the speculation. He did not wish to condemn Shirley to his transient lifestyle, albeit enviably luxurious. Some people did not adjust well to restarting their lives every ten years, finding a new career, new friends. It could be a lonely experience.

Then there was reproduction. Children. How could he ask her to take such a risk? If they proceeded the human way, she would most likely die before giving birth. He had read about an experimental procedure, in which a human female's eggs were fertilized with a male vamp's sperm, then implanted in the woman's womb after she had been turned. Unfortunately, so few embryos took. Something about a vampire woman's hostile womb. One laboratory was experimenting with ways to strengthen the womb and make it more hospitable. Another was researching the viability of using female vamps as surrogates for half-human embryos. That involved some genetic manipulation so that the embryo could grow. It was not yet considered safe.

He and Shirley would make beautiful children together, there was no doubt about that. And she would make a wonderful partner for the ages. Maybe, someday, they would have a chance. Donovan stroked his long, aquiline nose.

If she ever forgave him for pretending to be near death.

Marilyn pushed past Donovan's butler, Bryce, and tossed a magazine at him. She scowled, "Cripes, brother dear, even in death they're hoisting you onto a pedestal."

Donovan studied the cover of a local magazine and his mouth curled into a smile. The headline read, *Twenty-five Chicagoans we're actually going to miss.* On the cover, Donovan was poised in a leather jacket, a blue denim button-down, and form-fitting jeans. "Why, I think I look quite dashing, sister dear. What's the problem?"

Marilyn plopped onto the couch within striking distance. She was sure she was going to have to knock some sense into her brother. "Well, for one, you're not dead. This just pounds the nail into your coffin." She smirked. "How fitting for a vampire." She poked him in the arm. "However, that's not the point. If our community thinks you're dead, they are going to start jockeying for power. There could be an all-out war. You have to tell the Coalition you're alive, so they don't give your seat away."

Donovan laughed. "You're always bossing everyone around. Surely you can convince a bunch of nattering old men to stand down until I am really dead."

Marilyn glared at him. "You're missing the point, as usual. You may not be dead, but you are incognito. The authorities have declared that if you wake up, you'll most likely be in a vegetative state. Brain dead."

Donovan chuckled. "Any vamp worth his or her salt would see through that ruse. Vamps don't lapse into a vegetative state. It's impossible. My brain would spontaneously repair itself."

Marilyn punched his side. "Wake up, you idiot. They may suspect you're alive, but they have no real reason to honor that. Your disappearance provides a perfect opportunity for the Coalition and others to strip you of your power. Dad's nervous. Mom's nervous. *I'm* nervous. A Trait has served on the Council since *Grand'Mere* and *Grandpere* were turned. We have held that mantle for almost three centuries."

Donovan frowned at Marilyn. "What do you want me to do about it? I can't have one of the Coalition members revealing that this is all a masquerade. For all I know, one of those old duffers is involved. Besides, you forget. Dad is also a member. They won't push him around."

"Just give me your proxy. Let me hold your seat until you return. It's the only way."

Donovan threw back his head and laughed. "Talk about a power grab, dear sister. You just want a chance to be the first female vamp on the Coalition." He shuddered. "Oh, the damage you could do."

Marilyn hit him in the stomach.

"Will you stop assaulting me, sister? In human law, that's a crime." He gazed at her, his eyes assessing.

Marilyn sat back. He would see it her way. He was a Trait, after all. They ruled with a firm hand. Never ruthlessly, always graciously. But Donovan was the velvet fist in the family. He did not suffer fools or those guilty of betrayal. Marilyn pretended to study her manicure. When he didn't respond, she gazed at him from beneath her mascaraed lashes and inquired, "So? Do you agree?"

Donovan stood and began to pace. He strode across the floor, apparently lost in thought. When he reached the end of the room, he executed a military precise turn—no doubt learned while serving under Bonaparte—and came to a halt directly in front of her. He cocked his eyebrow and asked, "What's your end game, sister? What sort of damage do you intend to do?"

Marilyn's mouth fell open and she feigned innocence. "I just want to protect our position on the Coalition. Nothing more." She didn't need to tell him she intended to bring the Coalition into the twenty-first century, convince them to be more inclusive, share power with the female vamps. Hell, the females of her species had less power than humans. The network of laws that protected and promoted the rights of human women was staggering. She had more rights in the human world than in her own.

Donovan studied her. Then he executed another turn and paced some more. Finally, he stopped and pointed at her. "Fine. On three conditions—and I will require your agreement in writing, ascribed with the Vampire Oath—so consider carefully before you agree."

Marilyn refused to react. Instead, she said, "I will pledge under the vows of the Mediterranean Summit." The Summit had occurred in the mid-twentieth century. The result was a lengthy tome that consolidated all vampire families under one governing body, with standards of ethics and behavior, a system of laws, and penalties for noncompliance. One of the greatest penalties assessed was for the betrayal of family. That warranted exile and certain death. "Besides, what are you afraid of, brother? It will only be for a few months."

"Nonetheless, I will not be embarrassed or manipulated. So, in writing, you will agree that you have been given my proxy for a specific reason and a certain time period, to be determined solely by me. Also, I will retain the right to revoke your proxy at any time, for any reason. You will also agree to consult with me on every vote, and I retain the right to withdraw any vote when I return to power." His eyes narrowed. "I will not have you engaging in any behavior that violates my personal code of honor."

He paused. "And finally, you will share my proxy with another. Someone I know will keep your devious mind in check."

"Who's that?"

"Father."

"But he's already on the Coalition. Besides, he's in Tenerife."

"Not anymore." Donovan turned and smiled.

His father, the honorable Jonathan W. Trait, walked into the room, swinging an antique cane on his arm. He wore a very British morning coat, an affectation he had picked up in some royal court centuries ago. "Hello, my darling daughter." Jonathan tilted his head, his dark green eyes crinkled with amusement. "How's tricks?"

*Drat!* She never caught a break. Marilyn's eyes narrowed. "Father. Whatever are you doing here? Last I heard, you were mucking it up with the rich and famous off the coast of Spain."

Her father laughed. Jonathan Trait ran a hand through his thick gray hair, which was trimmed neatly around the crown. "Now what kind of father would I be if I did not rush to the side of my son, whilst he lay on his deathbed?"

Her mother, Gwendolyn, appeared behind him. Dramatically, she clutched her elegant pearls, which decorated a deep purple well-tailored dress, and said in a tremulous British accent, "Oh, I am absolutely devasted by the news of my son's ill health. I must be at his side and nurse him back to health.

Whatever it takes." She sighed dramatically and made as if to faint. Then she straightened and glared at Marilyn. "Unlike his loving sister, who seems more interested in usurping his power."

Marilyn opened her mouth to speak, but no words emerged.

Her mother cocked her coifed head, her blood-red lips curled up in a Cheshire-like grin. "Cat got your tongue?"

The high society matron smiled as she surveyed the Tribune headline. Donovan Trait's demise was all but certain. His parents had arrived to sit at his death bed, in the hopes of a miracle. She chuckled. Fat chance of that. She had shot the man in the head.

She had not intended to use a gun again in her third murder. How was she to know Robert Melton didn't drive? When she snuck into his garage in Highland Park, all she found was a Honda Civic, about ten years old. She knew someone as wealthy as Melton wouldn't drive that rust bucket. It must have belonged to a housekeeper or a grandchild. When she had arrived at his law offices early, intending to plant a small explosive device under his desk, fate had intervened. It seemed Melton was an early bird. She had almost fainted when he joined her in the elevator. Instead, she pulled her gun from her purse, stuck it between his ribs, and pulled the trigger. Then she had whispered, "Bye, bye," and exited at the next floor.

A bit of blood splatter had necessitated stashing her jacket in a nearby toilet tank. Her purse had been emptied to accommodate a bomb and detonator, so there was no room for bloodied clothing, so she found what she considered a safe place to dispose of it. The cops would check the waste receptacles for evidence, but not the toilets. By the time the jacket was found, the blood would most likely have washed away. She was confident it would not be linked with Melton's murder, and even it was, she was not the original owner.

After stashing the jacket, she left the public restroom and strolled out the front door. She was sitting in a cab before Melton's body had been discovered. It was a perfect crime.

She removed her blonde wig and scratched her scalp. Chemo had cost her a mane of fine brown hair, but despite all manner of scalp treatments, the regrowth was slow to begin. The wig was an annoyance, but it hid the obvious. That she was sick.

"My, my, aren't we casual today?" her husband said. He walked into the room and grabbed the front page from her hands. He sat and helped himself to a cup of coffee.

The matron waved him off. "My scalp is itching like a devil. And the wig isn't helping matters. If my baldness didn't make me look so pitiful and weak, I would just wear a scarf like other women. But that is hardly the image we want to project."

Her husband chuckled. "Of course, my fastidious little Jeannie must appear perfect at all times. I'm not sure this life has changed you for the better. I miss those days when you flounced around here in those tight, tight jeans and low-cut sweaters."

She gasped. "I did not flounce."

He cocked an eyebrow. "Of course, you did, my darling. You even went braless to make sure you bounced with every step. At first, I thought you had designs on my son. When you crawled into my bed, I was delightfully surprised." His eyes swept her body. "Unbutton that blouse."

The woman automatically reached for the top button.

"Oh, please, don't stop there. Let me see those marvelous tits you're so fond of flashing."

Suddenly nervous, she undid another button. At least the

cancer had not damaged her breasts.

"More," he said.

She reached for another.

The man's hand shot out and he tore the blouse from her body. Buttons flew onto the table and the floor. She stared at him in shock.

The man's face assumed a cruel smile. "Now that's a sight for these old eyes." He smirked. "I always like to be reminded of what I bought." He reached out and tugged at her bra, then tossed it on the table.

The woman's eyes rounded.

"Oh, don't play that innocent act with me. Did you think I didn't know you're sharing your favors? I see how my associates leer at you. Some of them even blush." He leaned over and sniffed. "Even now I can smell some man on you." He checked his watch. "A quickie before nine in the morning? Now that has got to be a record."

The woman lowered her head. Her lips quivered. There had been no other men. No dalliances or affairs. She had been too sick. Had he even noticed?

A single tear dripped down her cheek. She stood and removed her skirt. She stood before her husband in nothing but thigh high stockings and heels.

He grunted. "You've lost too much weight. You look like a scarecrow. You need to fatten up." He made a circular motion with his hand. Obediently, she bent over the dining table and spread her legs wide. She heard the sound of a zipper and felt the cold kiss of lubricant, a surprising concession to her illness. Without warning, he thrust inside her.

She tried not to smirk. Some women thought of England—she thought about nothing but revenge. He would pay like all of the others. She would so enjoy watching her husband burn, bound with leather handcuffs. Just like that movie where the woman set fire to the bed.

*First, we kill all the lawyers.*

*Burn, baby. Burn.*

# CHAPTER NINE: BOOM!

Bill stormed into Donovan's study and slapped a file folder into his hands.

"You're the only one living who's seen the perp. Look at those photos. Do you recognize anyone?"

Donovan opened the folder and took out the photos. He gazed at the first one, then the second and third. He stopped at the sixth. "I don't get it. What are these? They're photos of crowds."

"Surveillance footage from the scene of each crime. You. Criminal Courts. Wilson and Melton. Their office buildings. Had a probie review the footage an hour before and after each hit. We think we've found the woman, I mean, perp. Take a look. See anyone familiar?"

Donovan studied the photos from the Criminal Courts building. He tried to remember the face of the woman who shot him. "Truthfully, it all happened so fast. I did get some quick impressions. Blonde, matronly suit. Chanel, I think. So, wealthy. Attractive. Neat as a pin. As for her face, I've got nothing. One of those faces you tend to forget. That's why I wasn't very helpful when you had me work with the sketch artist. There was nothing about her that stood out."

"Please go through each photo. See if anyone looks familiar. My tech thinks he caught something. You've always had a sharp eye. Take a look."

Donovan picked up the first photo. He set it down and gazed at the second. He focused on the clothing of the women in each photo. His gaze flew back to the first. He put the two photos down and grabbed a pen, circling a head on each.

He moved to the next two photos, looking for the same hair, same shape, same style. Quickly, he circled two more heads. Donovan felt his heart quicken. Could it be this simple? Was this the woman who wanted him dead? He picked up the last two photos. This time, her hair was down. He frowned. Her clothing didn't match, but everything else was the same. He pointed to the last two photos. "Looks like the same woman, but different outfits. When did she have time to change?"

Bill shrugged. "She shot Melton in an elevator. Close up. Figured she got some blood spray on her. Dumped the jacket somewhere."

"It's the same woman in all of these photos, but all you've got is the back of her head. Do you have any photos of her face?"

"Nope. I was hoping these would tease your memory. Maybe a woman you rejected? Someone you've connected with at one of those fancy parties you're so fond of? I mean, you go through women like I go through underwear. Some of them have to harbor a grudge."

Donovan laughed. "And you think the women I date would also be attracted to Chuckie Wilson? Please. We did not fish in the same ponds. And Robert Melton is married. To a very nice woman in her sixties. His high school sweetheart, I believe. What about the crimes themselves? Any similarities there?"

"Both got the same text messages, but that's it. Wilson was poisoned. Someone delivered coffee and pastries to his office, left it on his desk. We later learned his personal assistant picked up coffee each morning from a stand in the lobby of the building. Finding coffee and a Danish on his desk was nothing unusual. He apparently assumed she had left it there."

"What about the coffee stand? Any surveillance footage there? Something you can compare to these photos? What about security footage in Wilson's reception area? Someone must have seen her."

"Ever seen Wilson's offices? The place is a zoo. All kinds of people coming in and out."

"Nothing in his office?"

Bill snorted. "You know better than that. Any hint of audio or video in a lawyer's office would get your hands slapped by the State Bar. Law firms have to be careful where they tape and what they tape. And even if there was a tape, they wouldn't release it to us. Attorney-client privilege trumps us."

'What about the elevator where Melton was shot? Surely they had surveillance in there."

"Nope. Nada. System was due for an upgrade, but it never happened. Budget cuts and such."

Donovan tapped the photos. "The back of her head isn't going to get you very far. It's not like you can distribute a *Be On the Lookout* with that. Besides, you can change hair. She could even be wearing a wig. It's more difficult to alter a face."

"True, but unless we can get a handle on the connection between you, Chuckie, and Melton, we have nothing."

"As far as I know, we have no clients in common. Different areas of practice, different clientele. We ran our client list against their filed cases and found nothing."

Bill sighed. "Maybe there is nothing. Maybe it's just some wacko chick who hates all lawyers. Maybe her father or an ex-husband was a lawyer and they did her wrong, so she's after some sort of twisted revenge. We've called in a profiler . . .

Donovan rolled his eyes. "With what little you've got, you're better off calling in a psychic."

"Yeah, well, sit tight. Technically, you're still near death. If nothing pans out, you may have to rise from the dead and serve as bait."

The Lynx stared at the results of all the searches he had run. Not a single match. He hissed. How was that even possible?

He stopped and pulled on the goatee that wafted from his chin. Somehow, he needed to get into the crime scenes. Take a look around. With his superior sense of smell, surely the killer had left some scent behind. A *parfum*, or soap, or even a shampoo. Those might not mean much to the humans, but to him they were everything. If he couldn't find the link through technology, perhaps he could find it the old-fashioned way. As a hunter in search of prey.

He frowned. It would be difficult to slip into a building staffed by humans. If he went in as a human, he would be stopped, recorded, perhaps searched. If he went in his natural form, he risked being shot. Humans did not take kindly to wildlife, especially the kind with sharp teeth and claws. They tended to shoot and ask questions later. Though he was fast in the jungle, there had been many near-disastrous encounters in the city. Several times, he had barely escaped with his life.

The Lynx tugged on his ear. *What to do? What to do?* He walked to a mirror that hung over the fireplace, gifted to him by his sainted mother, God bless her soul. She had tempted fate one too many times. Poor mother had run in front of a cab in the middle of the night, and smack! She had been left to die. By the time he had gotten to her, it was too late. She lay on the street flat as a pancake, the rats nibbling on her like it was their last meal. He shuddered. That had been . . . unfortunate. Unlike vampires, cats needed to shift to human form to heal. They did not spontaneously regenerate. When a cat was too weak to shift, they were toast.

The Lynx sighed. The only safe way to get into the crime scenes was as a passenger, in a purse, or something. His thoughts went to Molly. She was always toting one of those designer *suitcases* on her arm. Perhaps he could stow away there. The woman had a way of getting into places without notice. She was crafty and sneaky. And she was dating a cop, which meant she had connections. *Yes*. She was his best bet.

Now he just had to convince her.

He glided to his desk phone and allowed his long sharp nails to emerge. He extended his index finger and dialed. When Molly connected, he purred, "Molly, my darling. I need a favor."

The response was a loud groan.

"Molly?"

"What, cat? I'm busy. In a non-businesslike way, if you get my drift."

The Lynx gulped. "Um, I apologize? Perhaps, I should . . ."

Molly snorted. "You've already broken the mood. Spit it out. What do you need?"

The Lynx ran a finger over his wiry mustache. "Well, I was wondering. I was hoping. Oh, darn it, I need your help with a caper."

Molly giggled. "A caper? As in those little green things that come in a jar? Hate those things—"

The Lynx smirked. "Ha, ha. You are such a comedian. I need you to get me into the crime scenes undetected, so I can sniff around."

"And how do you propose I do that?"

"Stick me in your purse and carry me in. I have seen the size of your satchel. It could easily carry a petite cat like me."

"Have you looked at yourself in the mirror? There is nothing petite about you."

"Oh, sweet Molly. Don't toy with me. I am actually quite light in my animal form." He paused and grinned. "Unlike a big old lumbering brown bear."

"Careful, cat. You're asking for my help. You should be buttering me up."

*Oh, butter.* The Lynx's stomach growled. How he loved a luscious stick of cream and fat. He shook himself out of his butter-lust induced stupor and meowed. "I would really appreciate your help. You are one of the few weres of the larger variety that I can trust. Way too many see me as a potential meal."

Molly emitted what sounded like a groan. "Why do you need access to the crime scenes? The police techs have already been through them with a fine-tooth comb. They got nothing. What do you hope to find?"

"I just want to *sniff* around, see if I can find any consistent scents. Hopefully, the scent of the killer."

Molly harrumphed. "What good will that do?"

The Lynx rubbed his nose. "I am hoping I can find some clues as to who the killer is. For example, everyone assumes it's a woman, but what if it's a man? They say she's blonde, but she may be wearing a wig. And they claim she wears designer clothes. What if they're knock offs or something purchased at one of those consignment shops?"

"And your nose can detect all of that?

"Most certainly. My sense of smell is among the most acute in the animal kingdom."

Molly chuckled. "Most likely the places have been scrubbed. With bleach."

"Bleach bleaches. For a cat, it does not obliterate smell. It just irritates the nasal passages."

Molly hesitated. The Lynx heard a slight rustle as if someone had moved a sheet or blanket. His ear pricked up and he tried to home in on the sound. No luck. *Drat.* He was most curious about her lover.

"What's your timeline?

"Is this evening too soon?"

Molly spoke to her companion, attempting to mute their conversation. Unfortunately, The Lynx clearly heard every word. Hmmm. Her companion was named Joe. Apparently, he was working that evening. The Lynx hissed. He sounded quite manly. A deep, sensuous voice.

Finally, Molly said, "I'll pick you up at eight—as a Lynx. And I'll bring you back as a Lynx. No way do I want to see you naked."

The Lynx meowed. "Are you sure? My body is quite pleasing."

"Seriously, cat? A Bear and a Lynx? That would be like a Chihuahua trying to hump my leg."

"Ah, but my tongue can be quite pleasing . . ."

"Oh, please. Just shut it, cat. I'll pick you up at eight. Be ready."

Judge Shirley Magnusen was beside herself. Her grief over the loss of her lover, Donovan Trait, was so overwhelming that she was having trouble eating. Sleeping. Working. Life just wasn't worth living without him. Her despair was so great, all she could think about was joining him in the great beyond.

A single tear dripped down her cheek. No one would tell her where Donovan was. How could they deny her the opportunity to sit at his bedside? To hold his hand, stroke his arm, kiss his lips. She shuddered. No one wanted to die alone. Donovan should not have to die without friends either. He deserved to die around people who loved him and Shirley knew without hesitation that she loved him. When he died, she wanted to be there.

Yet no one knew they were lovers. With Donovan in a coma, he couldn't even request that she visit. Surely, someone knew something. Where he was being cared for. Whether his condition had improved. All the news shared had been dire, but spectacularly vague. Maybe the Chief Judge or the nice policeman who was handling the investigation would know. What was his name? William something. Yes, that was it. She crinkled her nose. What was his last name? Something with an *r*. Roost or Rouche. No, Roast. He had been at Donovan's last birthday soiree.

Shirley turned to her computer and typed *William Roast* into the search bar. As she waited for the results, she sat back in her office chair. Then she heard a thump and a click, as if someone had entered her outer offices. Probably the cleaning service. They were often noisy as they worked. They probably didn't realize she was even here. She stood, walked to the door, and called out, "Miranda? Sophie? Is that you? You can clean the outer offices, but I am still working—"

A woman dressed in a uniform, face mask, and goggles appeared before her. She knew the cleaners were all required to wear face protection now, so that was not surprising. Shirley smiled. "Oh, you must be new." She peered at the woman's identification badge. Then her gaze returned to the woman's face. "Oh, Miranda. Forgive me, I didn't recognize you. I've been so distraught about a dear friend of mine. He was shot, you see, and is clinging to life. He may die and if he lives, he will be a vegetable." She stifled a sob. "It is just so sad." Shirley straightened her robes. "Anyway, I'll be working late, so please make my chambers your last stop."

The woman nodded. Shirley turned and went back into her office, softly closing the door. She returned to her desk and gazed at the computer screen. Good, the search was done. She quickly scrolled through the results until she came to the story about Donovan's attack. She clicked on the article and leaned toward the screen. Yes, Detective William Roast. The article did not list his precinct. She went back to the search results.

There. The twenty-third precinct. Shirley wrote down the information. She checked her watch. Past ten. She yawned. Tomorrow would be early enough.

She stood and removed her robe, then reached for her coat and briefcase. When she walked to the door to her office, she frowned. The light was out. How had Miranda finished so quickly? Shirley opened the door and sniffed. She couldn't smell any cleaning supplies—that bleachy smell of the disinfectants they used. Instead, she smelled gasoline. Instinctively, Shirley slowly backed up and closed the door. She ran to the door of the courtroom and swung it open. Quickly, she moved to her court bench and ducked underneath.

Shirley heard a *boom!* Then debris fell from the ceiling. Finally, there was the smell of smoke and the crackling sound of fire. She peeked out from under the bench and a beam fell from the ceiling, striking her forehead.

Everything went dark.

# Chapter Ten: Reunited

Donovan paced back and forth across the library floor. He was furious.

Angrily, he shouted at Bill, "What do you mean they almost took out Shirley? What does that mean? Is she alive, barely alive, near death?"

"Do sit, darling," his mother cooed. Her eyes narrowed and she gazed at Bill. "Now who is this Shirley person and why is my son so upset?"

"He's been schtumping—," Marilyn began.

Donovan turned and glared at her. "Stop speaking like a third-class whore. And stop treating my Shirley like trash." He gazed at his mother. "She's the woman I love, Mother. Ye Gods, I was even thinking about asking her—"

His mother cleared her throat and cast a wary eye toward Bill, who was oblivious to the exchange. She stood and walked to her son, pulling him into a hug. "Okay, she's important to you," she whispered. "Now let the good detective tell us what he knows and we can move on from there." She gently pushed him into an armchair.

Donovan's eyes clouded with tears. *Dammit. Vampires don't cry.* Finally, he choked out, "Is she alive?"

Bill nodded. "She inhaled a lot of smoke and got hit on the head. Has a concussion. The doctors say she should recover fully, but it was touch and go for a while. All that smoke in her lungs, you know. But they got her into a hyperbaric chamber quickly. That saved her life."

Donovan sighed and buried his head in his hands. After a

moment, he raised his head. "Bring her here. I'll arrange for some private nurses to take care of her. I don't want her in the hospital alone. She has no family. *Only me.*"

"But you're practically dead," Bill protested.

"*She'll* be dead if news gets out that she's still alive." Donovan snarled. "Was it the same killer? Did she leave a note?"

"The judge's phone was destroyed in the explosion, so we are checking to see if there is any other way we can get access to her texts. I have to say, I'm surprised she got out alive. Something tipped her off and she ran in the opposite direction. I always knew Judge Magnusen was a smart cookie."

Donovan raised his eyebrows. He could barely control his emotions. "Is she under police protection now? What did you tell the press? What if the killer comes back?" The anger in his voice rose. "Are you doing anything at all to protect her?"

Bill held up a hand. He glared at Donovan. "I have been doing this job since you were in nappies, pal. Of course, she's in protective custody. And we told the press the same thing we told them about you. Critical condition, unconscious, undisclosed location."

"Then let me reassert my request. Please bring her here. I will make sure she has the best of care and keep her safe until the killer is found."

"Son, do you think that's wise?" His mother gazed at him. "You have enough to deal with right now. Why not let someone else—"

"Mother, don't you understand? I *love* this woman."

Marilyn rolled her eyes. "In my experience, you fall in and out of love at a moment's whim. So, you move Shirley in here. What happens if you tire of her and decide to move on? How will you get her out? You forget how easily *some* women get attached." She waved her hand. "They experience all of this and they get addicted to the luxury. They can't let it go."

His mother nodded. "She's right, darling." She cast her

hand outward. "This would enrapture any woman."

"Stop." Donovan held up a hand. "Just stop. Her near-death has clarified everything for me. I love this woman and I want to give her everything I have. *Everything*."

His mother grew pale. "But she's . . ."

Marilyn's eyes rounded. "You'll have to . . ."

Donovan turned away from them. He gazed at Bill. "I think staying here is the best option, don't you?"

Bill thumbed his lip. Slowly, he said, "Well, if the Judge agrees, I won't protest. But you're going to need to be sneaky about it." He pointed at Donovan's mother and sister. "Don't you two have somewhere else to be? The Judge hardly needs all the negative vibes you're shooting off. Perhaps the love-birds should be left alone."

Donovan smiled. Bill had never met his family, and he certainly didn't need to know them now. Meeting his sister again might get confusing, especially in her role as a judge. He would have to wipe his memory of them before he left the premises. Still, it was nice to have his support. He cocked an eyebrow and gazed at his mother and sister. "Exactly."

The high society matron glared at the Tribune. What was wrong with these lawyers? Were they superhuman?

One had survived a gunshot to the head, the other a bomb. How was that possible?

Thank goodness they were believed to be near death. Still, what if they didn't die? She would have to start all over again. She curled her lips in disgust. Both were being cared for at undisclosed locations. For all she knew, they weren't even in the city. God, they could be out of state. Iowa or Michigan or Missouri or Wisconsin.

She sneered at the newspaper. If they didn't die before she got to the end of her list, she would have the let them live.

Still, Trait was a vegetable, the judge was seriously burned. Maybe that was punishment enough. It was time to start planning for another death. She reached for her purse and pulled out the list. This one would have to occur away from the office. All law firms were on guard. She would have a difficult time getting past security. From now on, she would have to attack them in their homes or in public. That would be much more difficult. Most of these lawyers would be well-protected in their homes. Their deaths would require a little more ingenuity.

She studied the list. What she needed was someone whose car was not kept under lock and key. It would be easy enough to slip in at night and cut a brake line. She just needed to be sure she had the right car.

The matron smirked. Perhaps she should cut multiple brake lines. That would certainly bring things to a head much faster. Easily accomplished at the courthouse or other public venues. That would confuse the police. Could she pull it off?

She allowed her mind to wander, entertaining all the possibilities. Then she frowned. She had no problem with collateral damage, but her priority had to be the people on the list. And she had to strike while the police had no idea what was going on. Right now, they thought the killings were random. If they ever found the true connection between her victims, all would be lost. The gig, as TV cops liked to say, would be up.

The matron chuckled. No, she had to keep them confused. It was that confusion that kept them from seeing the truth. Perhaps it was time to change things up a bit. A different location. A different wig. Different clothes. She wanted them to believe that another killer had emerged. After all, most people hated lawyers. If two killers were on the loose, many might celebrate.

Ha! Time to get this party started. Oh, she so loved a party. Not the stuffy ones her husband dragged her to, but the ones of her youth. Drinking with abandon, dancing on tables and chairs, hooking up with strangers in the dark. That was when she had been free. Really free.

She grew dizzy at the possibilities, then realized she actually felt faint. Quickly, she placed her head between her legs and took deep breaths. *Damn this cancer. Damn the chemo. Damn the radiation.* Hadn't she suffered enough?

Maybe after she killed the lawyers, she would go after a few doctors . . .

The van pulled into the garage at Donovan's home and he hastily shut the door. To the casual observer, there was no reason to be suspicious. Everyone in this neighborhood had cooks, housekeepers, and a cleaning crew. To the interested observer, the van was clearly labeled. Its purported purpose was clear. Someone was merely cleaning his home while he fought for his life.

The door to the van opened and Donovan's gaze fell on Shirley, seated in a wheelchair. When their eyes met, he smiled and said softly, "Hello, darling. It is so good to see you."

Shirley's eyes grew wide, then she burst into tears. "Oh, Donovan. I've been so worried. They wouldn't let me see you. I thought you were going to die alone. It was awful." Tears ran down her face and she attempted to smile. "When they told me you were alive, I was over the moon." She swiped at the tears. Her eyes narrowed and her lips pursed. "I don't know whether to kiss you or kick in your manly pride."

Donovan instinctively stepped back, out of harm's way. He continued to smile. "As I'm sure Detective Roast explained, it was for a good cause. I couldn't tell anyone I was still alive, lest the killer make another attempt." He held out his arms. "Now come here and let me welcome you properly."

Bill helped Shirley stand. Donovan reached into the van, gripped her around her slight waist, and lowered her to the ground. She appeared a bit unsteady. Donovan frowned. "I think, for now, we are going to use the wheelchair, my love. No reason for you to move around until you're ready. Best keep you safe. I wouldn't want you to take another tumble. No, that won't do at all." He nodded at Bill, who lowered the wheelchair to the ground. "And if you can't use the wheelchair, I shall carry you wherever you want to go." He lowered her back onto the chair and tipped up her chin with a finger." His heart felt like it was going to burst with joy. "It is so wonderful to have you here." He kissed her tenderly.

Bill groaned. "Okay, okay, you love birds. We need to make like your house is being cleaned. My crew will handle turning the lights on and off in the rooms. You two settle in one place and stay out of our hair."

Donovan nodded. "I promise we'll be out of sight until morning. We will retire to my bed chamber and get reacquainted."

Shirley smiled at him. "I'd like that." She titled her head. "You have so much to make up for."

Donovan took her hands. "And I shall, my dear. I promise you."

Bill cleared his throat, obviously uncomfortable. "Judge, where would you like us to put your bags?"

She giggled. "In Donovan's *bed chamber*, of course."

Bill's face reddened, but he nodded. "Okey dokey. Let's get everyone inside."

Donovan stepped behind Shirley's wheelchair and pushed her to the foyer.

Shirley gasped. "Oh, Donovan, this is a gorgeous home. Every painting, every piece of furniture, even the Oriental rugs, shout your name."

A man chortled. "They should. When he was a child, he

destroyed half of them. He didn't give a hoot about tradition."

Donovan turned the wheelchair so Shirley faced an older man in a crisp black suit.

The man bowed and in an elegant British accent said, "Bryce Lawton, ma'am. Butler, furniture repairman, and chief bottle washer."

Shirley smiled at him and grasped his hand. "It's a pleasure to meet you, Bryce. Donovan has told me so much about you. How you found him in the forest, unconscious after he had taken a fall from a horse, and how you smuggled him food at boarding school. I want to hear all of your stories."

Bryce chuckled. "I'll bet he didn't tell you that he stole *my* horse from the stable because he thought riding a pony at eight was unmanly. He's lucky he survived that one. And the only reason I smuggled in food was because he was so poorly behaved, his headmistress kept sending him to bed without his supper. His mother was beside herself. He was lucky the headmistress had a soft spot for me and permitted me to visit my former charge, for *counseling*. Separation anxiety, you know." He smirked.

Donovan blushed. "Well, make sure you tell her the whole story. How you taught me to cheat at Scabby Queen when I was five and Whist when I was ten. I was a regular card shark. Headed for a life of crime, all thanks to you."

Bryce grinned. "Aye, you were a quick study, even then. My biggest error, though, was teaching you how to win over the ladies. Taught you how to be a right proper gentleman and that has taken you far. Too bad you behave like such a scoundrel. In fact, my lady, you may want to reconsider your association with this reprobate. I wouldn't trust him any further—"

"Oh, I can assure you he's been reformed, Bryce." Shirley smiled brightly at Donovan. "Unless I've been misled, he recently became a one-woman man."

Donovan dropped down to his knees and lovingly took Shirley's face in his hands. "Yes, Bryce, I am a changed man. This woman is the love of my life. And I almost lost her."

"And I almost lost *him*," Shirley cooed.

Donovan gazed into her eyes and kissed her. "Never again, my darling. We shall never again be parted."

Bryce cleared his throat. "I'll see to dinner, then." He left the room.

Donovan kissed Shirley's eyes, her nose, her cheeks. He pulled back and studied her. "You look tired, my darling. After a proper nap, perhaps we can continue this discussion."

Shirley yawned. "I am tired, sweetheart. My lungs aren't fully healed, so breathing is a bit difficult. A nap just might do the trick."

Donovan stood and swept her into his arms. "Then a nap you shall have."

"Donovan, I'm not a child. I'm too heavy to carry."

He shushed her. "To me, you're light as a feather." He carried her into his library and settled her onto a settee. He grabbed a blanket from another chair and wrapped it around her, then urged her head onto an embroidered pillow that read, *Sharks don't attack lawyers for a reason. They don't eat their own.* A gift from Molly.

Shirley sighed and quickly fell asleep.

Bryce brought a tea tray into the room and settled it on Donovan's desk. He smiled at Shirley's sleeping form. "She's quite a lady, that one," he said softly. "I hope she's strong enough for what lies ahead. You light up in her presence, you know. Why, you almost seem human. It's so strange to see the normally stoic, controlled Donovan Trait filled with so much passion, so much love." He chuckled. "It's very unvampire, yet so wonderful to see. You've been lonely for far too long. And it would be nice to have some children around. Three hundred years is a long time without the magic of children."

Donovan nodded. "She is special. I only hope she can accept who I am, *what* I am. If not, I shall have to wipe her memory, wipe all thought of me from her mind. That would be devastating." He sighed. "Even though there's still a big question mark over children, I can imagine building a family with her. A child in her belly. A child at her breast. A whole flock of children crawling all over our laps. That would make me very happy." He gazed at Shirley. "This woman makes my heart beat stronger. My days so much brighter. She is pure joy. And you're right, it feels strange. Unexpected and strange. My emotions are all over the place. It's overwhelming and distracting. If this is what humans experience, no wonder they are so undisciplined. I almost feel out of control."

Softly, he said, "I almost lost her. That can't happen again. I must protect her."

# Chapter Eleven: Revelations

The Lynx peeked out of Molly's purse as she headed into an elevator. This was the third and final stop.

He had been right to visit the crime scenes. By the end of this adventure, he would know the killer's scents. Not only her perfume but her shampoo, her conditioner, her nail polish, her moisturizer, her makeup, her clothing, her lingerie. After the second crime scene, he had several scents locked down. For example, although she wore a wig—yes, that scent was unmistakable, dead human hair had a cloying smell—there was also the slight scent of some sort of hair product. He needed to isolate it.

This final visit should do the trick.

Although it was way past closing time for most offices in this building, someone tried to enter the elevator with them. *Now that won't do.*

Molly coughed. Loudly. Then she sneezed. She waved off the person with, "I think I'm coming down with something You might want to take the next one." She continued to cough until the person stepped back.

The elevator doors hissed closed. The elevator began to move, then suddenly lurched to a stop. The Lynx popped his head out of the purse.

Molly pulled the zipper open. "This is the last crime scene. She shot the guy in this elevator."

The Lynx jumped down to the elevator floor. He sniffed his way along the seams in the walls and floor. That was where scents hid, untouched by chemicals and the human hand. He stopped when he caught a whiff of human blood. Yes, this was where the victim has landed. He traversed a circle around the blood, searching for a scent of the perp. There, along the back. She had been standing behind the man. *She shot him in the back? That was so . . . cowardly. And so human.*

He crawled up the wall, his nose confirming the scents from previous crime scenes. He caught another whiff. What's this? More blood? Ah, the victim's, not the perp's. He frowned. How had blood gotten this far up the wall? Then it became clear. The woman had gotten blood on her clothing. How had she hidden that?

He forced out his human shape.

Molly quickly covered her eyes. "Geesh, cat. That is not something I need to see, ever. Put some clothes on."

The Lynx smirked. "Sorry, my sweet. 'Tis the fate of the Lynx to appear sans clothing in human form." He preened, then rubbed his hands together, making no effort to hide his private parts. "We need to find the closest ladies' room. The killer caught blood splatter, which means she may have ditched at least some of her clothing."

Molly nodded. "I do remember Donovan saying when she left, she was dressed differently from when she entered. They just assumed she had shoved her jacket in her purse. If she ditched part of her clothing, we might finally have a real clue. She covered her eyes. "Put the fur back on and let's get to it."

The Lynx shifted back to his animal form. He meowed, then leaped onto Molly's arm and crawled around her neck, across a breast, and back into her purse.

"What the hell was that?" Molly sputtered. "A new way to feel me up? You couldn't just jump into my purse?"

The Lynx meowed. She knew he couldn't respond after shifting. Perhaps if she had been more polite and lowered her purse for him, he wouldn't have been required to get all . . . touchy-feely. He butted his head against her.

Molly frowned. "Fucking perv." The elevator began to

move.

The Lynx heard the door open and close, and someone entered the elevator. Then it moved again. Molly shoved The Lynx's head further down into the purse and zipped it.

The Lynx didn't react. Not when others were around. He knew his little bear had a temper. It was what made her so enticing. His cat's claws had probably pinched a bit when he had meandered across her body, but what was a cat to do? It hadn't been malicious, merely a bit of curiosity. It wasn't like he could feel up his sweet WereBear while in human form. She would cut his paws off. He shuddered. That would be disastrous.

The elevator bell sounded and the door opened, then Molly began to move. The Lynx waited patiently. He knew she was headed to the bathroom. He heard a door swing open, then shut. Molly unzipped her purse and his eyes blinked in the sudden, unnatural light. God, he hated fluorescent bulbs. They tinged everything with a greenish cast. This time, Molly lowered her purse to the floor and he jumped effortlessly out onto the floor.

He strolled to the garbage receptacle and sniffed. It smelled surprisingly fresh. He walked into a stall. There was the scent of the victim's blood, but it was faint. He moved to the next stall. Stronger. The next stall was taped off. A sign said, *Toilet broken. Maintenance called. Please use another stall.* The Lynx slipped under the door and sniffed. He moved around the toilet. Had the perp attempted to flush an article of clothing? No. The smell was coming from the tank.

He meowed loudly, and when Molly's head appeared over the stall door, he rose on his back paws and tapped the tank.

Molly frowned. "You think it's in there? That's going to be a mess."

The Lynx meowed again. Surely, she understood he couldn't extract anything while in animal form. A large plastic bag flew over the door and landed at his feet. He hissed and shifted. Apparently, his sweet teddy bear was unwilling to get her hands dirty. Carefully, he removed the lid from the tank, setting it on the toilet seat. Inside the tank, some sort of material was wrapped around the plumbing. He sighed. It was wet, and no doubt some blood had already washed away. At least it was something. He muttered, "I wish I had gloves."

"Quit your carping," Molly snapped from outside the stall. "You can wash your hands when you're done. Now hurry up, before someone else comes in."

The Lynx grabbed the plastic bag and turned it partially inside out. He maneuvered his hand under the lip of the bag and used it to pull at the wet mass. After a few tugs, it came free. He held it above the tank and allowed it to drip. Then he dropped the material into the bag and sealed it. He wasn't sure what the item was, but it smelled of the victim's blood. That was all that mattered.

The Lynx pushed the bag under the door and it disappeared. He shifted back into his animal form and slipped back out of the stall.

Molly held the bag up and gazed at it curiously. "Geesh, cat. That's a hell of a way to ruin a jacket." She shoved it in her purse and frowned. "Not sure you're going to fit in my purse, now. Besides, this thing weighs a ton. I'd need a cart to move you, too." She pulled the zipper closed. "You're going to have to dodge all the humans out there and make a run for it. Luckily, I parked nearby." She opened the door and with an evil grin, said, "Now scat!"

The Lynx arched his spine and hissed. Then he ran as if the devil himself was blessing his ass with tongues of fire.

Donovan took Shirley's hands into his and gazed into her

eyes.

She had recovered swiftly from the blast. She no longer needed his care. However, she did require his protection, at least until their killer had been caught. It was time to tell Shirley the truth. The *whole* truth. While Donovan was sure Shirley loved him, she loved only what she could see, what she thought she knew. Would his confession change things? Learning that her lover was a vampire could elicit several reactions. Terror. Shock. Repulsion. Anger. Or maybe, acceptance.

Donovan didn't expect acceptance. Humans had a hard time with that. He just hoped that over time, Shirley would realize that the love she had for him—and he for her—trumped the excess baggage created by his heritage. After all, it wasn't like he was a shifter—half-human, half-beast. He was almost fully human, with a few genetic tweaks. Over history, vampires had worked hard to fit into the human race. Though they valued the unique qualities they possessed, they had developed a need for companionship and even, love. Since their numbers had decreased, it had been natural to gravitate toward similar life forms.

Shirley arched a thin blonde eyebrow. "What, darling? You look like you have something to say."

Donovan brought her hands to his lips and kissed each palm. "I do, but now that the time has come, I find I am having trouble finding the words."

Shirley smiled. "There isn't much you could say that would shock me." She winked. "God knows, I've certainly explored every nook and cranny of your—"

"Shirley, I'm a vampire."

Shirley giggled. "Really? That's the best you can come up with?" Her lips turned up into a grin and she giggled again. "Oh, Donovan, you are such a delight. Now you could certainly dress up as a vampire. What woman doesn't fantasize about being taken by a hot, sexy creature of the night?" Her smile grew wicked. "And there are rumors that when a vampire bites, the ecstasy is out of this world. Earth-shattering, even." She shuddered slightly. "What woman could turn that down?" She patted his hand. "Unfortunately, we all know that's a myth." Shirley's blue eyes narrowed. "Why would you tell me something like that?"

"Because it's true."

Shirley glared at him. "Really, Donovan," she huffed. "That's not funny. Everyone knows vampires don't exist. They are fiction." She pulled her hands from his grasp and studied him. Her eyes began to fill. "If you want to break me up with me, certainly you can come up with something better than that." A single tear trailed down her cheek.

*Ye Gods.* He had never expected tears. Tears were just so . . . human. He had never learned what to do when a woman cried. Donovan slid off the settee to his knees and again took her hands in his. "Oh, my sweet woman. I don't wish to end our relationship. I want to make it permanent. But to do that, I must let you see the real me. Everything I am.

"I love you. Not the simple kind of love that brings candy on Valentine's Day, but the kind of love that is deep and true. Everlasting. The kind that brings laughter and joy, kids and dogs, a home out in the country with a white picket fence. I want it all with you, darling, but unless you know the whole truth, that can't be." He pulled a linen handkerchief from his pocket and dabbed at her tears.

Shirley blinked. She threw herself at Donovan and landed in his lap. "Oh, Donovan, I love you, too," she sobbed. "So much it hurts. I miss you the minute you leave me until the minute you return. When I thought you were near death, I was beside myself. I didn't think I could survive. I wanted to die with you." She took Donovan's handkerchief from his hand and delicately blew her nose. "But I still don't understand why you would tell me such a crazy story. It's as if you are trying to scare me away."

"If I was truly a vampire, would that frighten you?" He re-adjusted Shirley in his lap and kissed her softly. He moaned at the taste of her luscious lips.

She gazed into his eyes. "I'm not sure. I'd like to think love can overcome everything. I mean, if you look at vampirism as some sort of deficit or disability, then it is part of who you are. Take that away and you aren't you, are you?"

Donovan sighed. How could he make her believe? He gently sat Shirley back on the settee and walked to his desk. *Where the family Bible sat.* "Let me show you something, darling. Join me, please." He extended a hand. Shirley stood and walked to him, hesitantly taking his hand. He opened the cover of the book and pointed to the first page, which contained the family tree. It was rather sparse after his birth, but the dates were clear. Donovan pointed to his name. "What does this say?"

Shirley peered at the page and her eyes settled on his name. "Donovan Jonathan Trait, born May fifth, seventeen twenty-five." She blinked and moved closer. "An ancestor?"

Donovan shook his head. "No, that's me."

Shirley stared at him. "But that would mean you're hundreds of years . . ." She wobbled on her feet and Donovan's arm went around her waist.

"After a period of time, vampires don't age, darling. Once we pass puberty, we can choose when to stop the aging process."

Shirley continued to stare at him, "But you don't look a day over . . ."

"I chose to stop aging at thirty-five. Some wait longer. My parents, for example, stopped aging at 50 . . ."

A confused expression crossed Shirley's face. She gazed at the Bible page and traced the lines to his parents. She turned pale. "That would mean they're . . . they're . . ." She daintily slid out of his grasp and he caught her before her head hit the carpet. Her eyes closed.

"Oh, damn," he muttered.

Shirley's eyes opened slowly and her gaze settled on Donovan's face. His stunning, artistically sculpted face. The face of the man she so loved.

He gently stroked her cheek. "There you are, my darling," he crooned. "You've had a bit of a shock."

*Oh, yes. That he's a vampire. Or rather, he thinks he's a vampire.* She didn't even know how to classify that delusion. It wasn't like he could bite her and drain her blood. Because if he could, she would die and that would be . . . she squirmed. And the thought of her love flying around the room as a bat was so . . . She shuddered. If this was a joke of some kind, it simply wasn't funny. Though Donovan made her giggle and smile, he wasn't a comedian or someone given to practical jokes. He poked fun at the humor in life. So why was he trying to convince her that he was a vampire?

Donovan leaned toward her and settled his lips on hers. They were such sensual lips. Soft, yet demanding. His tongue swept into her mouth and she joined him in an erotic dance. Surely a man who kissed like that wasn't a . . . No, the world could not be so cruel as to make her fall in love with someone who was mentally impaired.

Her hands reached to cradle his face and his kiss deepened. The small flame that lit in her belly began to grow, and desire overtook her. Shirley sighed. Donovan's hand stroked her breast through her clothing, his lips kissing her neck. Her mind clouded with lust.

A single thought poked through the haze. If he was a vampire, wouldn't he bite her?

Donovan's hand drifted down to her leg, inching her skirt

up to her waist. Then he slipped it between her legs and gently pushed them apart. Without a word, he tore her panties from her body and stuffed them in the pocket of his suit coat. Then his mouth slowly descended. He kissed, he sucked, he probed, he pinched, his movements growing frantic as Shirley moaned and shuddered. His tongue lapped at her mons and then he gently nipped her tiny button.

Shirley screamed and her body spasmed. Her mind filled with the bright white of ecstasy. Donovan held her still as she trembled. She pinned him to her body, her legs holding his head to her body. He had once again transformed her into a whimpering puddle of need. Breathlessly, she whispered, "Oh, Donovan, I love you so. If only you weren't a . . . I mean, if only you didn't claim to be . . . a vampire."

Donovan gazed at her, his expression somber. Gently, he pushed her legs away from his head and worked his way up her body. As he held himself up over her, his gorgeous blue eyes met hers. "But I *am* a vampire, Shirley. There's nothing either one of us can do about that. If we are to be together and build a life, at the very least you must accept that. Otherwise, we have no future."

Panic overcame Shirley. Tears flowed unbidden. Was she so taken by this man that she could entertain his fantasies, his delusions of mythical proportions? Wouldn't it be best to walk away? To pretend he had never made such an outrageous confession? As she gazed at him, she knew she could no more leave this man than cut off a hand. She loved him too much. Her heart had shattered when she thought him near death.

As much as her mind fought her, her heart and her soul were bound to this man in ways even she didn't understand. It was almost unbelievable that she, Shirley Regina Magnusen, the iron maiden of the Chicago Circuit Court, was irretrievably in love. With a man who claimed to be a vampire. *Damn.*

She smiled through her tears. "It's ridiculous, you know. Being a vampire. You could no more feast on the blood of maidens and shift into bat form than I could eat babies for breakfast. How do you expect me to believe that?" She shook her head. "That's ridiculous. Tell me you're being ridiculous. Tell me you're joking."

Donovan carefully kissed both of her cheeks and murmured, "I'm afraid . . ."

"If you're a vampire, show me your fangs. In all the time I've known you, I've never seen fangs. You've never even tried to bite me."

Donovan sighed and sat up. "First, let me explain a few things to you. The vampires you read about in books and see in films are myths. Vampires have roamed the Earth for many, many centuries. Those myths were born of the need to explain the unexplainable. There was a time when we were forced to feed upon humans and animals, but advancements in science have dispensed of our need for human blood. In fact, I find human blood rather foul. Now we take a daily supplement, specially prepared for those of our kind. That enables us to eat the same foods as humans." He gave her a half-smile. "Though I will admit that I still prefer my steaks on the rare side."

Shirley stared at him. "I don't understand. If that's true, then why even tell me?"

"Because I want to marry you, and vampires can't marry humans, especially if we desire to have children . . ."

"I still don't understand . . ."

Donovan remained silent.

A thousand thoughts raced through Shirley's mind. He couldn't marry a human? Why the hell not? He was pretty much human, except for the fangs of course—if he had them. He was almost as human as she. And what was this about babies? For God's sake, they hadn't even discussed children yet.

Unless . . . A cold dread filled her and the reality dawned bright. "Oh." Shirley's eyes rounded. "Oh. I have to become . . . become a vampire to marry you?" She paled. Her head began to swim. "That's, that's—"

"A lot to ask, I know."

*No! He can't be serious.* In all the books she had read, she would have to die before being reborn as a vampire, and the risks were great. There was no guarantee she would wake up. She stared at Donovan. Was it possible behind that mask of the perfect gentleman lay a bloodthirsty monster? No, that was too horrible to contemplate. Finally, she managed to choke out, "So, you bite me, drain my blood, I die, and am reborn as a vampire?"

Donovan rubbed his forehead. A perplexed expression crossed his face. He started to speak. Then he stopped and sighed. "There are two types of vampires. Some are born, others are what we call *turned.* In the past, that involved the process you just described. But as I said, science has made significant advancements and we have evolved. The process is now a mere outpatient procedure. Once a month, you receive a vampire's blood by IV, and over time, it will replace your human blood. That stimulates certain changes within the body. For example, your senses are heightened, and your lifespan will be extended indefinitely. Once your blood begins to reproduce the cells of a vampire, you have been officially *turned.*

"There is no death involved. At worst, you may have nightmares for a while. Your mind may not fully accept your new reality and fight it. But the process will turn you into one of us."

"That sounds too easy. There's no pain? No thirst for blood? No fangs?"

Donovan shook his head. "Much of that has been dealt with by modern science. Well, except for the fangs, and I will get to that. Physiologically, humans are very close to vampires. We are humanoids, but our DNA is different. Our internal thermostats tend toward the cold. We rarely get hot or sweaty. I am sensitive to light, but a good pair of sunglasses deals with that. We simply have a few more cells than humans. Most of those are performance-enhancing—better vision, better hearing, a more discerning palate, increased strength." Donovan smirked. "And an unrelenting libido."

Shirley frowned. "Then what's the downside?"

"Well, vampires have problems reproducing, and unfortunately, carrying a vampire fetus can pose some health risks, but we're working on that. And my fangs do come out when enraged or aroused. During sex, they may emerge and I may bite you, leaving a mark. That can be hard to explain to a human. But the bite also bonds you to the one you love. It is not intended to harm, but to display affection."

"You've never bitten me." Shirley narrowed her eyes. "Are you saying you've never been aroused by me?"

Donovan laughed. "Oh, my sweet woman, how could you even think such a thing? You know I adore you. When you're in my arms, my thoughts are only of you."

She huffed. "Then why have you never bitten me?"

"For me, a bite is a very intimate act. I would never dream of biting a woman without her consent. It's not something you can discuss over dinner."

Shirley didn't know what to make of that. Was he really that disciplined? Was Donovan's moral code so rigid that he could withhold his pleasure out of consideration for another? He was the consummate gentleman, sure. That was why women flocked to him. But in her experience, most men only pretended to be a gentleman until they reached the bedroom. Then they became beasts. Still, upon reflection, Donovan had always been an indulgent, considerate lover. He actually seemed to gain pleasure from giving her pleasure. When they were together, it wasn't all about him. It was all about her.

Suddenly, Shirley reached an epiphany. He was the perfect man, for her. Fangs or not, she wanted a life with him. She no longer cared that it would never be normal. Really, what woman would complain about stopping the aging process—watching friends and family pile on the wrinkles and gather gray hairs while she remained untouched for all time? If she was being honest with herself, a life with Donovan had no downside. She was woman enough to accept that. And the first step was to give her consent.

Shirley reached for him and pulled his face towards hers. She kissed him, trying to infuse all of her love into that one kiss.

Then she purred, "Donovan, bite me."

# CHAPTER TWELVE: REDUX

Donovan jerked away from Shirley when Bill burst into the study.

"She got another one," he shouted. His face was red, his ugly tie coming out of its knot. "Dammit, she assassinated another lawyer."

Their faces slightly flushed, their clothing somewhat askew, Donovan released his hold on Shirley and cocked an eyebrow. "Have you never learned to knock? We were—"

"Who was murdered, detective?" Shirley asked, quickly adjusting her skirt. "Was it another judge?" Shirley took Donovan's hand as if to calm him.

Bill shook his head. "No, this time it was a law professor. At Northwestern University." He pulled a cell phone from his pocket and fiddled with it. "Professor Warren T. Roberts. Either of you know him?"

Shirley gasped. "He was my contracts professor when I was in school. Most of my law clerks have been referred by him. He's become a colleague and a good friend." A troubled expression crossed her face. "Why would anyone want *him* dead? He was tough on first-year students but fair. And an excellent teacher. The students adore him. Each year the first-year students put on a musical revue to honor him. It's hilarious and has become a great fundraiser."

Bill gazed at Donovan. "What about you? Do you know him?"

"I know *of* him. Remember, I graduated from Harvard Law. The only connection I have with Northwestern is through clerk hiring. Each year, my firm interviews several students from NU for our summer law clerk program." He frowned. "Could that be the connection? Law clerks?"

Bill stroked his lips. "Might be." He shrugged. "At the moment, the killer's list of victims has us pretty confused. There are no obvious connections. Is there a possibility that you both had the same person serve as a clerk?"

"It's very likely," Shirley said. "We both hire men and women from Northwestern. Donovan hires first and second-year students. I hire third years and recent graduates. It's feasible that someone who clerked for Donovan also clerked for me."

Bill typed in a note on his phone. "What are the chances you shared a clerk with the others who have been murdered? Wilson and Melton?"

Donovan grimaced. "Not likely. Our practices are too different. And I don't think Wilson hired law clerks. He hired mostly paralegals. There are few actual lawyers at his firm. The paralegals handle most of the case preparation and negotiation, and Wilson collects a fat fee. There's almost no legal work involved. Melton's firm is more upscale. His clerks have to be in the top five percent of their class and they are required to complete courses in labor and employment law. My clerks are geared more toward criminal defense."

"And my clerks must be multi-taskers" Shirley added. "I mostly handle civil cases, and that covers a lot of ground. It's hard to see my clerks going to Wilson or Melton's firms. Most move into civil litigation. Still, anything's possible, I suppose."

"What's the best way to find out?" Bill asked. "You two can't do it. You're supposed to be close to eating dirt."

Donovan winced. Eating dirt indeed. "Just call each office and ask for a list of clerks over the past five years." He paused. "No, make that ten years and throw in Shirley's old firm,

Stewart & Stevens. She was there for six years before becoming a judge three years ago. We can't just assume this has something to do with her judgeship."

Bill nodded. He gazed at the couple. "I have to ask again. Is there anyone you can think of who would have it out for you? Anyone you disciplined or fired? Maybe someone who was angry that they weren't hired?"

Shirley leaned into Donovan and smiled up at him. She returned her gaze to Bill. "We rarely discipline or fire anyone. It's much easier to find them a job elsewhere. A place in which they might be better suited, like a corporation or government agency. And most are smart enough not to burn any bridges in the legal world. Getting angry with us is simply bad form. Remember, we are potential references, and even though our recommendation may be somewhat lukewarm, that is much better than a negative one. How one leaves a law firm is just as important as how one enters."

"No names, no incidents, come to mind?" Bill asked.

Shirley tilted her head. "You know, it may not be someone we hired. It's just as likely to be someone we *didn't* hire. I'm quite sure we don't keep track of all applicants. We get hundreds each year. It wouldn't be prudent to save each and every resume."

A look of frustration crossed Bill's face. "Dammit, there has to be some connection we can find."

"Maybe you won't find the connection until you find the killer, Bill," Shirley said. "Only the killer knows why each of us was selected. It doesn't have to make sense to us. It only has to make sense to her. For all we know, there may have been one isolated event at which she believes we all slighted or offended her. Not sure how we could even sort that out." She tilted her head. "How did Professor Roberts die, Bill?"

"Someone cut his brake lines. Went right into the NU parking garage in broad daylight and snipped them. We caught a glimpse of the perp on the security tapes, but he or she looked nothing like the other one. Tight jeans and a T-shirt, a black ponytail pulled through the back of a Cub's hat. Skinny thing, too. She slid right under the car. Was out in five minutes. Knew where the cameras were, too. We never got a glimpse of her face."

Bill frowned. "We're lucky the professor got out of downtown before his brakes went out, otherwise we might have had a mess on our hands. He could have plowed into students or pedestrians while leaving work. As it was, he was on Lake Shore Drive just entering Evanston when his car spiraled out of control. He wound up hitting a tree dead on. He was killed instantly."

A look of horror crossed Shirley's face. "That poor man. His last few moments must have been filled with such terror. Losing control, knowing he was going to die . . ." She shuddered. "Poor Ren. He didn't deserve that."

"And there was a text, like the others?" Donovan inquired.

Bill nodded. "That's the only reason we think it's the same perp. She changed things up with her appearance and a different MO, but same text, same words. She wants us to know it was her." He scowled. "Basic police science is failing me now. There is almost nothing for the profiler to work with, and those photos of the perp are going to get me nowhere. Without a face, I'm at a dead end.

"I may never find this woman. Hell, she may not even be a woman. I don't even know the color of her hair. She's good. *Too* good. She understands how cops think. What we look for when we investigate. Hell, she could be one of our own. God knows, we have plenty of cops who flunked out of law school." He threw up his hands. "I can't anticipate her next move. I can't get into her head. Dammit, I need to figure out how her mind works."

Donovan nodded. He smiled at Shirley and took her hand.

"We'll do what we can, Bill. Obviously, we want her caught. We'll check our employee lists and see if there have been any crossovers. If there are, we'll let you know."

Bill stood. His shoulders slumped in apparent defeat. He gazed at them, then he waved and walked out.

The high society matron emitted a giggle of excitement. The law professor's death had been easy. A little too easy. Nothing had gone wrong. No one had even noticed that she had readjusted the cameras in the parking garage. The police must be pulling their hair out. *Ah, the tricks you learn from cop shows.*

She picked up the Tribune and pulled it closer. Carefully, she read the story again. When she finished, she frowned. There was no mention of Donovan Trait or the lady judge. It was as if they had fallen off the face of the earth. She paged through it. Surely, there was some mention somewhere.

Her husband stepped into the room and without a word, grabbed the newspaper out of her hands. She ignored him, and instead picked up her teacup and sipped. She studied the man she had married years ago. He hadn't aged well. Initially, there had been a physical attraction. He wasn't homely by any means. Most women would find him appealing. Distinguished, even. Until he opened his mouth. That was when the rough edges—that southside of Chicago upbringing—became apparent. All the fancy cars and designer suits couldn't disguise that. Still, money excused a multiple of shortcomings, and they were swimming in it. It made him tolerable. For now.

She softly cleared her throat and nodded at the paper he held. "There has been another death. A law professor this time. I imagine the rank and file is getting nervous, wondering who's next."

Her husband laughed. "We're guessing it's some batty

housewife with delusions of grandeur. One of those wallflowers so plain her husband ties her up and puts a hood over her head so he can fuck her. I'm not a bit worried. She seems to be going after the media hogs, the people who seek publicity. That's not my thing. Eventually, she'll settle down and just disappear."

She nodded, forcing herself to remain polite. "Have you heard anything about the two victims who didn't die? Trait and that judge?"

He shrugged. "Only what they tell me on the news."

"No word on the street, reports from his friends?"

The man frowned. "Jesus, woman. Do you have the hots for Trait?" He laughed. "You are way out of his league. Why would he be interested in a cougar like you?"

She scowled. "I never said I was interested in him. Just wondering if he has died yet. I haven't seen anything in the paper for a while. Everything has been about that judge that got blown up."

He snorted. "Squirrely Shirley? It'll be nice to have her off the bench. The bomber did us all a favor with that one. She's a little too by-the-books for my liking. Everything is black and white with her, when the law is really shades of gray."

She giggled. "Shades of gray?" She began to laugh. "Oh, that's too funny. Perhaps someone should write a book about kinky lawyers."

The man glared at her. "I can assure you there is nothing kinky about the law." Then he grinned slyly. "Lawyers, however . . ." He spread his legs and pointed to the floor. As he fumbled with his zipper, he ordered, "Assume the position, darling. Maybe if I keep your mouth busy, it won't spew such nonsense."

Slowly, the matron lowered herself to her knees, hiding her disgust. His time would come. And it would be the happiest day of her life.

The Lynx dutifully recorded all of his impressions from the crime scenes and hit the key to activate his evidence sorting program. It prioritized his findings by weight of importance. Given the number of exclusive products he had sniffed, it should be fairly easy to narrow down the suspect pool. Not everyone could afford those cosmetics, and some were specifically tailored to the user. All he had to do was break into the records of the vendors to identify the recipients. Then he could cross-index those with other search findings.

While his software worked, The Lynx turned to the search Molly had requested. While he had found multiple names that had some connection with more than one of the victims, no one person had connections with all five. More troubling was the fact that all but one of the suspects were men. Maybe the perp didn't have a personal gripe with the vics. Maybe they were motivated by something that occurred to someone else. A spouse? A child? A friend? A lover, perhaps? The possibilities were endless. But that was the *only* possibility that made sense.

The Lynx wheeled his office chair over to a different computer. He had run a background check on all of the names with multiple connections. The Lynx mewled. It would take forever to peruse these files. He tapped his hairy chin. How could he cut this list down?

The Lynx scrolled through the material, searching for any disqualifying factors. First, he eliminated all of the suspects who had not attended Northwestern University Law School. Good. Down to fifteen, but still too many. He continued to scroll. Something had caught his attention the other day. What was it? He continued to scroll. *There.* He called up the search bar and asked, "How many still living?"

Eleven names popped up. Then the Lynx typed, "How

many dead?" Six names popped up. He sighed. How could a human be living and dead? He chuckled. Unless they were a vampire. He sobered. Anything was possible, but if the killer was a vampire, she would have known how to kill Trait. No, poison and guns were the tools of a human.

He studied the names of the dead. Slowly, he read through their death notices. One died in a car accident. Another from a genetic heart defect. Four cited no reason. The Lynx frowned. No mention of the cause of death was usually someone who committed suicide. He knew humans were a bit prickly about that. For religious or other reasons, they tended to push suicides under the rug. Still, not everyone published death notices for family members. There was some expense involved. Newspapers made money for publishing obituaries. That meant there might be other possibilities.

The Lynx fingered the hair in his ears. Well, at least he had narrowed the current list down to four. He rolled back to his other computer. Damn. Two of the people had no known connection to Trait and the other two had no connection to the judge. And only one was a woman. A woman who was dark-skinned, but of uncertain ancestry. Obviously, he was missing something. A factor that linked one of them to both.

Time to call his sweet Molly. Maybe she could help.

# Chapter Thirteen: Break-through . . . Sort Of

Donovan sipped his cup of tea and gazed through the patio doors at his very English garden.

How he loved those new UV ray protected windows. Here, he could enjoy his garden without donning sunglasses. The glass did all the work, allowing light to filter freely into the room, but blocking the UV rays that threatened his sight. It had been a long time since he had felt the searing pain of exposure to sunlight. He just wished he could sit in his garden without sunglasses. The tint of the lenses interfered with the colors of the flowers and the green of the plants.

He sighed. At least he could enjoy the scents. He chuckled. And the absence of pesky insects. His blood did not attract mosquitoes or hornets. It repelled them. That was something he must pass on to Shirley. She always complained about the black flies and mosquitoes on the lakefront.

His moment of peaceful contemplation was interrupted by his butler, Bryce.

"Excuse me, sir," Bryce said. "Detective Roast is here to see you."

Donovan nodded. "Show him in, and bring in some donuts and coffee, please. Bill does love his donuts."

Bill strolled into the room, a smirk on his face. "Donuts? Really, Trait? How about some of that Kringle you always have around?" He patted his stomach. "The wife has insisted I stop the donuts, but she didn't say nothing about Kringle."

Donovan chuckled. "What brings you here, Bill?"

"Just checking in. Wondering whether you and the judge have come up with anything."

Donovan shook his head. "I've got somebody working on it, but so far we've got nothing. I was hoping the police had made more progress."

Bill frowned. "We've got one smart perp here. Even the profiler is puzzled. We can't figure out the connection between all of the victims. And she's all over the place with how she kills them. Most serials kill the same way, even stage the vics in the same pose. That makes it easier to profile them. With this scattered approach, the only way we'll know if she's done killing is if she tells us or disappears." Bill's eyes narrowed. "She's one pissed off killer, but other than the fact she hates lawyers, we've got nothing."

"Ever consider she is one, or is married to one? A lawyer, that is."

Bill laughed. "Sure. That was our first thought. But that and fifty cents gets us nowhere. I imagine there are a lot of frustrated lawyers, even failed lawyers out there. And plenty of unhappy wives. Not just in Chicago, but everywhere." Bill rubbed his forehead. "Hell, Chicago could be her first stop. Maybe she's just getting warmed up. Maybe she's going to hit up New York, L.A., Seattle, Atlanta, and Dallas, then move on to London, Paris, and beyond."

Donovan scoffed. "That's a lot of anger."

"Well, until we figure out what's causing it, we can't stop her." Bill's phone rang and he reached into his pocket to retrieve it. He fumbled with the instrument, then brought it to his ear. "Yeah?" He was silent for a minute, then his face paled. He mumbled an obscenity and disconnected. "Gotta go. Someone just set a state senator's house on fire."

Donovan took a deep breath. "Our perp?"

"We don't know yet. We don't even know if anyone is

dead. Those guys spend most of their time pissing someone off."

"Wait. Who is it?"

"Garrett O'Shaunessy. Know him?"

Slowly, Donovan nodded his head. "He's a member of the Chicago Bar. Actually won a few pro bono awards before he got elected." He frowned. "Now I'm even more confused. I know him, but that's the extent of our relationship. He was with Legal Services, then the Public Defender's Office. We have had no professional or personal connection at all."

Bill shrugged. "No surprise there. Nothing about this case makes sense."

"But Bill? He had a family. O'Shaunessy had a wife and several children, I believe." Donovan buried his head in his hands. "Ye gods, now she's killing children."

Molly waltzed into The Lynx's library and sniffed. "Smells like wet cat in here." Molly held her nose. "What on earth did you do?"

The Lynx cackled "I skinned a bear. They can be quite . . . um, fragrant."

Molly thrust her hands on her hips and scowled. "Seeing as how you called for my assistance, insulting me will get you nowhere. Now what do you need? I had to get a new purse after carting you around half of Chicago. I couldn't get the smell out. So if you're looking for a chauffeur, you're out of luck. I can't afford another purse."

The Lynx preened and a sly smile crossed his face. "I'm close, my dear. I have four possible links." He straightened the papers on his desk. "I need your boss and the delightful Judge Magnusen to peruse a few files, look at a few photos. See if they ring any bells."

"Are any of them women?"

He shook his head. "That's not the issue, because these people aren't the killer. One of them is the link to the killer. They are the reason the murderer is on the rampage. I just need to figure which one. And once I do, we'll be able to find the killer."

Molly scowled. "How do you figure? Isn't that doing it ass-backward?

"Think about it. Why do people kill? Usually, it's out of some sort of twisted revenge. Sometimes, on their behalf. Sometimes, for others. My best guess is that this time, it's the latter."

Molly rolled her eyes. "That makes no sense."

"*Aw contraire*. It makes perfect sense. You see, I have managed to connect the vics to four people, and those four people have one thing in common. They're all dead. Which means the killer could be a sister or mother, a girlfriend, or a former lover. They could even be a former teacher or friend. Maybe a nanny. Whomever they are, I believe one of the dead persons is the reason someone is killing lawyers. It's the only logical conclusion."

"And out of all the information I gave you, you found only four possibilities?"

The Lynx hissed. "I found fifteen possibles, but I eliminated most of them."

Molly raised her eyebrows. "May I ask why?"

"They're still alive. And if they're alive, chances are, they'd be doing the killing themselves. Of the four who are dead, the cause of death isn't available. All signs point to suicide. What better reason for murder than to avenge the wrongful death of another?"

Molly frowned. "You're taking a big leap, cat. At the root of suicide is some form of mental illness. Depression or something like that. How can all of these people be blamed for one person's depression? It's chemical, not situational."

The Lynx held up a finger. "However, when a person in the depths of depression, they aren't thinking rationally. Anything could be a trigger. Rejection. Bullying. A personal loss. A financial loss. Bad news. What if a series of events, all precipitated by the victims, just pushed someone over the edge?

"If you had a family member who was rejected or bullied throughout their lives and ultimately took their own life, what would be your first instinct? Would you not be out for blood? For revenge?"

Molly stared at The Lynx, her mind racing. Yep, he could be right. It was the only thing that fit. Someone was killing lawyers for revenge. The link could be the person the victims had intentionally or unintentionally harmed. Working at a law firm wasn't for the weak or the faint of heart. New lawyers, in particular, were treated abysmally. If they weren't overworked, they became the scapegoat for every error a senior lawyer made. They were treated like chum.

It wasn't pleasant, but law firms needed to separate the wheat from the chaff. It was imperative to discard those who could not perform under rigorous conditions. Molly considered. How many lawyers had been found unworthy and doomed to an unsuccessful career? Word got around in the legal community. Lawyers talked. Enough rejections. Enough pink slips. The doors would close. The only option would be public service or opening your own practice. A devastating result after surviving law school and the bar exam.

Molly gazed at The Lynx. Softly, she said, "Sadly, revenge, even for someone else, makes sense. There is a reason so many people hate lawyers. Some save lives, others destroy them. While I can't imagine Donovan or the judge acting badly, to a troubled mind, there's no telling what might be the nail that seals the coffin."

The Lynx handed her four folders. "I need the judge and Trait to take a look at these four people. Maybe one of them will trigger a memory. I need anything they can give me. Even if they are uncertain. One of these four is the key, I am convinced of it."

Molly carefully studied the labels on each folder. Devan White. Lucinda George. Matthew Donahue. Marshall Davis. She frowned. Something stirred within her memory. She quickly opened each file and gazed at the photos. There. Him. He had begged and begged for an interview, but there were no open slots. Nothing in his records indicated he had what it took to work for Donovan anyway, so she had held firm. She scrunched her nose in concentration. He'd had a fiancée, maybe a baby on the way? A horrifying thought seized her. Was she responsible for the attempt on Donovan's life?

She reopened the man's file. No obituary. Molly pointed at the man's face. "This one. I'll bet it's this one. He had a fiancée, a pregnant one. Find out what happened to them. She could be the key." She groaned. "Dammit, I wouldn't even let him in the door. This one is all on me."

Molly sat at the round table and placed the four files in front of her. "Before you open those, we need to have a chat. Because if I'm right, you are being blamed for something you knew nothing about."

She pulled out a file and set it before Donovan. "We found four possible connections, each one dead by their own hand." She tapped on the folder. "This one I remember because he was so persistent, so desperate. Each time he called, I turned down his request for an interview. He just didn't fit our criteria. He wasn't what we needed." She nodded at Donovan. "Open it. Do you know him?"

Donovan opened the folder, and his eyes grew wide. "Matthew Donahue? I *do* know him. Quite well, actually. He was one of the students assigned to me through the Bar's mentorship program." He frowned. "I thought we parted on good terms." He leafed through the file. "Wait a minute. You said he was dead? That can't be right. I remember seeing a birth announcement in one of the suburban papers. He was married and a father. He wasn't the brightest lad, but he got a job right out of law school, a good one I believe. At some corporation." Donovan gazed at Molly. "My door is always open to those I mentored. Why would you deny him access?"

Molly flushed. "He never mentioned he knew you. I'm sure of it. He kept requesting an interview. I thought he wanted a job."

Donovan rubbed his forehead, messing up his smoothly combed hair. "I hate to think this was spurred by a mistake. Besides, he had the number for my private cellular phone. Why didn't he just contact me directly? I would have no reason to avoid him. Matt can't be the connection. I'm sure of it."

He turned to Shirley and pointed to the photo. "Did you know him?"

Shirley studied the photo. She began to shake her head but stopped. She paged through the file. "I didn't know his name, but I think we're in the same legal fraternity. I must have inducted him. I have conducted the same ceremony for the past five years. But why would he want to harm me? Getting into a legal fraternity is a good thing. You certainly don't murder people over it."

Molly blew out a breath of frustration. "You're sure there's nothing more? You didn't turn him down for a clerkship or maybe, a recommendation?"

Shirley shook her head. "My secretary handles all of that. She and my current clerk go through the applications and provide me with five names for each opening. Sometimes there's one opening, sometimes there's two. It depends on the budget. I look at the files and select two to interview. Then I render a decision. My participation is almost minimal."

"Can we find out if he applied? Does your secretary keep

the resumes of the candidates?"

Shirley shrugged. "It's possible, but it's not like I can ask. I'm supposed to be in a coma, remember?" She gazed at Donovan. "We need to get Bill involved. He could probably make information requests about all four of these people. Obviously, he needs to start with the secretaries. They would have pertinent information. I just hate to think all of this is about something about which we had no knowledge. That any of these lawyers died because of a decision we had no control over. That's just horrible."

Molly flushed. Finally, she said, "My job is to make Donovan's job easier by dealing with things that don't require his attention. I like to think I'm good at it. This . . . this makes me question everything."

Donovan placed a hand over hers. "You do a great job, Moll. I have no complaints. This killer isn't thinking rationally. Even if this is related to Donohue, don't make any assumptions. We have no way to know what precipitated the killings. Right now, all we've got is a guess.

"Now, let's take a look at the other three files."

# Chapter Fourteen: A Quist of Fate

Detective Bill Roast whistled as he watched the home of the Honorable Dudley Horacio Quist, Esq. God, he loved it when he got a lead.

The murderer had screwed up. This time there was a witness. A neighbor looking out of her window at twilight had seen a woman hustling down the street, away from the victim's home. Suspicious, she had snapped the woman's license plate. Shortly thereafter, the house burst into flames.

The car was registered to Quist, but the driver could have been almost anyone related to or employed by the LaSalle Street attorney.

Bill's partner, Harry Finley, yawned. "Been pretty quiet, Bill. All the lights are out. Either they've gone to bed or no one's home. Maybe we're wasting our time. How long do you plan to sit here?"

Bill grunted. "Until our back-up arrives, then I need to start working on the responses we've received from the secretaries and personal assistants. See if I can figure how Quist or someone related to him fits in."

Finley sipped from his supersize coffee. "You sure that the fire at O'Shaunessy's house is related? You never did find the guy's phone, so there was no text like the others. It may not be related."

Bill nodded. "My Spidey Sense is kicking in and it's telling me that it is connected. Getting the perp's license place is going to break this case. I can feel it. I just need to figure out who was driving the car at the time of the fire."

Finley placed his coffee in a cup holder. "Remind me why we're not knocking on the door and asking? Seems like a simple question with a simple answer."

"The Chief is tight with Quist. I thought it best that the question come from him. He declined to pose it. Said the woman reporting the plates didn't see the driver near O'Shaunessy's home. In his words, *just because a snoopy old bat saw someone she doesn't know walking down the street doesn't make the driver a killer*." Bill rolled his eyes. "He said if Quist had been seen, he might have asked, but there were a lot of cars on the street. Anyone of those drivers could have set the fire."

Finley snorted. "He may be right, but again, simple question, simple answer." He scratched his bald head. "Well, if Quist isn't the link, you have five daughters, a mother, a wife, a housekeeper, a cook, and numerous mistresses to choose from. Anyone of them could have been driving that car. You need to check whether any of them have a connection to the vics."

Bill shook his head. "That's going to take a while. This perp is smart. He or she has been careful to avoid the usual traps. Every murder has been different, there is no weapon of choice, all the crime scenes have been clean."

Finley's eyes narrowed. "Hey, maybe every murder has been different because all five of the daughters are involved. They could each be relying on their weapon of choice." His voice grew more animated as his excitement grew. "Maybe they've got Daddy issues and that's why they're killing lawyers. Maybe he's abusive or worse, a molester. That could drive someone to murder."

Bill sighed. Without any real clues, anything was possible. "We don't need more speculation, we need less, Harry. We've got to narrow this down."

Finley nodded. "The killer seems to be getting bolder. They're risking collateral damage now. What were the chances that O'Shaunessy would be the only one home?" He shuddered. "Cripes, if the wife and kids hadn't been at their cabin in northern Wisconsin, we could have had four more people in the morgue." Finley punched Bill's shoulder. "But if anyone can figure this out, you can. You've got enough people working on it. Someone has got to find something."

The middle-aged matron peeked out from behind the curtain, gazing at the street below. The unmarked police car was still there. How had they managed to find her? Did they know she was the killer, or were they there for other reasons?

She giggled. Maybe she should just march out there, tap on their window, and ask. Or maybe she could send Mildred out with coffee and donuts. Cops and donuts went together like a hot dog and mustard. She giggled again. She could spike the coffee with one of her sleeping pills, or maybe a laxative.

She felt her husband approach.

"What's so interesting out there?"

She turned toward him. "An unmarked police car has been parked up the street since last night." She gazed at him. "Not sure who they're watching. Maybe the Quists or the Sheltons. Is there some reason they might be watching us?"

He looked out of the curtain and scowled. "I can't think of a single reason the police would have me under surveillance." He hesitated. "Unless the Chief thinks I'm being targeted by that serial killer."

He pulled his phone out of his coat pocket and dialed. After a few seconds, he said, "Ralph? I've got an unmarked sitting up the street. Did you send me some watchers?" He was silent for a moment, then walked back to the window. "It's got Illinois plates, but I can't really read the number from here. Maybe you can send someone by to check? If it's the killer, I certainly don't want to go out there. Give them a clear shot." He chuckled. "Yeah, not smart. Well, let me know what's going on. If that's your guys, they're making my wife nervous." The man smiled as he disconnected the phone. "Not to worry my dear, one way or another, they'll be gone soon."

He walked to a sideboard and poured a cup of coffee. Then he sat down at the dining room table and studied the front page of the Tribune. "Damn, that killer is getting sloppy."

The woman joined him at the dining table. "What do you mean?" she asked as she settled into a chair.

"Well, she isn't going after only one target anymore. She's going after families. It's like she doesn't care who she kills, as long as she hits her target. That professor's car could have hit another car or even a pedestrian. Hell, in downtown Chicago, he could have plowed into a crowd. We're lucky there weren't more casualties. And now, Senator O'Shaunessy's home. What if his family had been there? They all could have been burned to a crisp. That family was very lucky."

"But not so lucky for the Senator," she said softly.

The man gazed at her, his expression unreadable. "My point is a man would never be so sloppy. Male serials are precise. They make clean kills. Women are sloppy by nature. They aren't confident in making their kills." He took a gulp of coffee. "Just another thing women can't get right."

The matron bristled. She had not been sloppy. She'd had to mix things up so she wouldn't get caught. If anything, she had been creative. She had thrown the police off the scent. She rose from her chair and walked to the coffee urn, filling her cup. "I'm sure the killer knew that the Senator was alone."

"Maybe, though I doubt it. Who knows how the criminal mind works?" Her husband looked up from the newspaper and gazed at her. "Speaking of which, did you get your car into the shop?"

She nodded. "Dropped it off yesterday. I couldn't get the darn thing to start the day before."

The man shrugged. "That car has always been a bit tricky. Maybe it's time for a new one.' Without waiting for an answer, he went back to reading the newspaper.

The matron hid her smile. She had pulled in next to the mechanic's bay that contained the Quist's BMW. It had provided the perfect alibi. She had simply removed the car from the lot after the shop was closed and returned it before anyone was the wiser. She chuckled to herself. Not sloppy at all.

Donovan watched The Lynx carefully as he prowled around Donovan's library.

The Lynx examined the books, then an assortment of antique toys. "My, my," he purred. "You have quite the collection here. Some of these toys must date back to the eighties. The eighteen-eighties, that is."

Donovan peered at the Lynx over the top of his reading glasses. The shifter was the slippery sort. While he was indisputably brilliant, he was also a little too sneaky. He had been in Donovan's library for less than five minutes, and already Donovan was wondering if he would have to ask his butler, Bryce, to search the WereCat's pockets before he was allowed to leave the premises. "Eighteen sixties, actually. I have a fondness for Civil War history. Each of those toys tells a story. I imagine for the children of that time, the war was very frightening. Toys were a distraction from reality. The toys provided solace the family couldn't."

The Lynx merely nodded. "Well, perhaps you'll allow me to trace the ownership of your toys sometime. Try to document their path to the present. You're right, each has a story, and it would behoove you to document it before it's lost."

Donovan nodded. "Perhaps. After we have resolved the matter of my intended murderess."

The Lynx padded across the carpet and sat in an intricately

designed Louis XV armchair. "I got the information requested on O'Shaunessy and added it to the others. Of the four prior candidates, he was connected to only two, Marshall Davis and Matthew Donahue. You've had a chance to review the material I gathered. Any conclusions?"

Shirley entered the study pushing a tea cart. She picked up a tray with a small teapot, cups, and saucers, a small pitcher, and a glass of a white beverage. Shirley gazed at the Lynx. "I assumed you'd prefer a glass of cream to a cup of tea. Correct?"

The Lynx purred. "What a sweet, considerate lady you are." He fingered his mustache and smiled. "I don't suppose—"

"She's taken," Donovan snapped. "By me."

Shirley huffed. "Donovan, really. I am not *taken* by anyone. I am not a piece of property." She set the tray on Donovan's desk and bent down to kiss his cheek. "I will forgive your poor choice of words this time. We're all under a lot of stress." She smiled at The Lynx. "More appropriately, Donovan and I are in love and are considering marriage. So, no, your display of courtly behavior has no impact on me." She smiled sweetly. "However, I do wish you luck in your search for love. It *is* a many splendored thing, as they say."

The Lynx cocked a spindly eyebrow. "Well, since you are only *considering* marriage, Molly knows where to find me if things fail to reach fruition."

Shirley's eyes rounded, clearly surprised. She giggled. "Well, I doubt there's much chance of that."

Donovan cleared his throat. "Yes, well, be that as it may, we aren't here to discuss marital status. Shall we return to Donahue and Davis?" He gazed at Shirley. "Shirley and I know both these men, but our interactions with either offer no cause for murder. I was Donahue's mentor and we had a productive relationship. I know that Molly blocked a few of his calls, but if he had been desperate, he could have called me on my cellular device. He had the number. And Davis was a first-year intern at my firm as part of a class at Northwestern. He was one of ten students. There was no job prospect involved, they were merely there to get a sense of what was involved in law practice. Each was assigned to an associate and followed them around for a few months. The only time we had any interaction was at social events. I believe there was a welcome party, an activity with the associates – rock climbing as I recall – and an end of the semester pub crawl. I was at the welcome party and made a few remarks, but other than that, I had no interaction with the interns," He grinned. "I declined the opportunity to climb mountains and consume cheap beer. I'm too old for either."

Shirley snickered and patted his hand. "Indeed, you are, darling."

The Lynx delicately set his glass of cream on an end table. "But each did have some connection to you. Whoever the killer is, she is acting on their behalf. This is clearly about vengeance, the question is vengeance for what? Even your failure to interact with them, or their belief that they were owed more personal attention, could have served as a trigger." He gazed at Shirley. "What about you? Do either of these men ring a bell?"

Shirley nodded. "According to my secretary's records, each applied for a clerkship, but neither made the cut. They simply didn't have the grades. They weren't interviewed by my clerk, so they were never interviewed by me." She frowned. "I get hundreds of applications each year. We have strict rules about who gets interviewed. First, we reduce the pool to ten and request legal writing samples. Then my clerk selects five and asks them to prepare a short brief. That list is narrowed down to two and I interview both. Neither of these men made the initial cut. There was no hope of a clerkship.

However, I did meet Donahue through my legal fraternity. I am quite sure I was the lawyer who inducted him as a member."

Donovan held up a hand. "Those aren't the only opportunities for contact, though. Both Shirley and I have taught continuing legal education courses. We attend Bar Association events. Just because we didn't consider them for hire or work with them on a case doesn't mean there wasn't any further contact. We just have no recollection."

The Lynx tapped the arm of the chair. "Let's leave that for a minute. They are both dead. Unless they left detailed diaries, we may never know how you are involved. What we should be focusing on is who in their personal realm is capable of unleashing a killing spree?"

"How can we possibly know that?" Donovan asked

Shirley gazed at The Lynx. "Donovan is the only one who can identify her. The woman I saw was wearing a mask. I just assumed she was a regular worker."

Donovan sipped his tea, his eyes thoughtful. "We need to share this information with Bill, too. Maybe he has some leads that can help."

The Lynx arched his back and hissed. "*The police?* Please. They can't know I'm involved. My methods of information gathering are a bit unconventional, and to the police, may be considered unscrupulous. I barely skate within the lines of propriety now. I really don't need their attention."

Shirley raised her eyebrows. "You mean you're a hacker?"

The Lynx bowed his head but said nothing.

Donovan waved him off. "That's neither here nor there. I'm not going to give him your research. I am simply going to suggest two possibilities. But first, get us the headshots of female family members, maybe close female associates. We need to know if there's the slightest possibility a family member is involved. If we have that, he won't have to know where the information came from. He'll just assume Molly dug it up from our files."

The Lynx meowed. "It would not be unlike her to claim credit for my work anyway. Bears are so . . . insecure. Everyone assumes they're dumb, like that cartoon, Yogi something. So they have problems with low self-esteem. However, if it will keep the cops off my back, I'll allow it. Then Miss Molly will owe *me*." The Lynx grinned, a grin tinged with mischief.

Shirley snorted. "She's dating a cop, you know. A deputy sheriff. Make a move on her and he'll run you through every criminal database available. Then he'll stalk you until he finds some dirt he can use against you. Her Joe is very protective. Best you keep your hands to yourself."

The Lynx sniffed. "*Pull-ease.* He may be all big and bulky, but I've got superior intelligence. And everyone knows the brain is the most important sex organ."

Shirley shook her head and giggled. "Maybe, but you have to back it up, *physically*."

Donovan stared at Shirley and blushed.

Shirley laughed. "Oh darling, not to worry. Even without a brain, you'd be irresistible." She leaned over and kissed him.

The Lynx hopped to his feet. "With that, I'll be on my way. Seems to me you two love birds need some alone time." He smiled slyly at Donovan. "Just remember, seduce her with your brain and she'll be yours forever." He waved a hand. "Enjoy." He turned and daintily slid out of the room.

# Chapter Fifteen: Bites . . . and Things

Donovan pulled Shirley close and nuzzled her neck. She moaned distractedly and grabbed a hand of popcorn from a bowl, popping it into her mouth, one kernel at a time.

As he watched her cherry red lips close around each little puff, her little pink tongue darting out to catch the salt and butter, Donovan's heart swelled. As did other body parts. To him, Shirley was the whole package. She was bright, beautiful, and irresistible. On the bench, Shirley was a tiger. She had no qualms about ripping an errant attorney to shreds. But here, in his home, cuddled up on his bed, watching one of her favorite old movies, she was as content as a pussycat. She was simply a delight to behold.

Donovan knew he had been lucky to find her. Ye Gods, it had taken more than three hundred years. Unfortunately, Shirley had not yet consented to his proposal of marriage. She hadn't even mentioned it. He didn't even know if it was still under consideration. He, Donovan Strait, the big bad vampire lawyer, was afraid to ask. After centuries of taking, this was a new predicament for him. Women threw themselves at his feet. He was never without female attention. Yet none of that really mattered. He had never wanted or needed anyone before. Now he wanted Shirley. And he needed her. His life would be empty without her.

Donovan nuzzled her neck again, making his arousal evident. "Darling," he crooned. His hand grazed her breasts as he planted tiny kisses down her neck. When Shirley moaned, he slid his hand inside her silk robe and caressed her mons.

Gently, he kissed her, then pushed her onto her back, spilling the bowl of popcorn onto the floor. Donovan nipped and sucked his way down Shirley's lush body, stopping when he reached the apex between her thighs. Lovingly, he lapped at her lips and inserted a finger to caress her G-spot. His teeth settled around her tiny button and he bit down.

Shirley bucked off the mattress and shouted his name. She thrashed and shuddered, her growing pleasure apparent. Donovan continued to lap at her pussy, delighting in her coos and moans. As her movements became more frantic, Donovan thrust his fingers more aggressively into her channel. Shirley writhed and began to beg, "Donovan, please. Please . . ."

Donovan chuckled and crawled back up her body. "What do you need, my darling?" He feasted on her neck. "Tell me what you need." His mouth moved to her breast and he allowed his fangs to scrape her nipple.

Shirley gasped. "Please . . . inside me. I need you now."

Donovan was nothing if not indulgent. He parted Shirley's legs and slid inside of her, watching her face carefully as his cock expanded inside her. Unlike humans, a vampire's arousal unleashed a trio of reactions. The fangs. The desire to bite. And the supernatural expansion of their penile member. However, it took a disciplined vampire to discern the difference between pain and pleasure, and Donovan was determined to give Shirley nothing but unquenchable bliss.

Shirley moaned. "Oh, Donovan. That feels so . . . exquisite."

Donovan moved smoothly within her, taking care to caress all of the bundles of nerves. He smiled as Shirley's body writhed with delight and rose to meet each thrust. His heart swelled when her eyes glazed over and her pleasure became apparent.

Shirley gasped, then shuddered. She screamed his name.

Then her eyes slowly closed and her face became infused with ecstasy. She climaxed noisily, then slowly melted into the sheets. After a few moments, her eyelids slowly opened and she smiled dreamily.

Donovan stayed inside Shirley, her pulsing pussy gently easing him back from the brink. When he regained control, he pulled out and lay down beside her. He kissed her lips, his heart filled with overwhelming emotion. *This. This is what it means to love and be loved.*

They lay quietly, kissing and stroking, drifting in and out of consciousness. After a time, Shirley gasped and sat up. "Oh, Donovan," she said. "You didn't bite me." She scrunched up her face in confusion. "Why didn't you bite me?"

Donovan gazed at her. How could he explain his need for her commitment before he allowed himself to lose control? The thought of sinking his fangs into her luscious body filled his nights and days. Yet he knew unleashing such intense passion would result in an explosion of pleasure so addicting, he would lose all restraint. The ecstasy went beyond the bounds of human understanding. It catapulted every single nerve into an uncontrollable flame of desire that, when fully satiated, elevated lovemaking to a whole other plane. It resulted in a bonding so complete that only death could break it. And once that bond was created, the words *until death do us part* took on a much more dire meaning.

If Shirley willingly bonded with him, and she died, his heart would be truly broken. It was the only other way that a vampire could die. Of a broken heart.

While some vampires semi-bonded without impunity, never committing to one mate, Donovan had been taught that the bond was sacred and should not be entered into lightly. So he had waited for the one woman who set his heart and mind on fire. Shirley.

Donovan sighed. "I find I cannot unleash the vampire in me without knowing that the bond we create will last forever, my darling. You have given no answer to my marriage proposal. Or to the turning necessary to live out our life together. I have never created that bond with any woman, vampire, or human. I have waited patiently to find my true mate." He kissed Shirley, swiping her soft lips with his tongue. "That woman is you. There will never be another."

Shirley's eyes filled and she blinked rapidly. "Donovan, I don't ever want you to discount my love for you. It is all-consuming. I cannot imagine living without you." She closed her eyes and took a deep breath. "The problem is, I am damn scared. Frightened out of my wits, actually. There is so much I don't know. So much I don't understand. You are asking me to step off a cliff without a parachute, and I don't know if I have the courage."

"How can I assure you? What will it take to bolster your courage?"

A single tear ran down Shirley's cheek and she swiped at it. "Dammit, I'm ready to bawl like a first-grader."

Donovan smiled at her indulgently. "I will do anything to make you more confident about your decision to join me. I suspect if you had asked me to become human, I would be just as unsettled."

Shirley's eyes widened. "You can do that? Become a human? Oh, that would solve—"

Donovan shook his head. "Unfortunately, that is something scientists have explored for centuries. A *cure* for vampirism, as if it's some sort of chromosomal defect. That's like expecting someone to cure Down's Syndrome or Autism. We have learned to manage vampirism, to adapt to life among humans, but we are not human. We never will be." He smiled slightly. "I am quite sure we are a more superior species."

He took Shirley's hand, kissed each knuckle, then sucked

on each fingertip. "I won't force you to turn, Shirley. It must be your decision. However, I could introduce you to women who are vampire-born, as well as some who have been turned. Anonymously, of course. Nothing face-to-face. They won't risk exposure. But I am sure they would be available for an interview via computer. I could set up a special chat room. An untraceable one. You could ask questions and they could respond without impunity. Would that help?"

Shirley nodded, fighting back tears. Then, as if turning on a faucet, the waterworks exploded and she began to sob, burying her head into Donovan's chest.

He rocked her gently. He was well aware that Shirley's decision was life-altering. There were so many considerations, so many adjustments. It was a lot to expect of anyone, human or otherwise. Fate had dealt them a difficult hand, but he had no doubt they could overcome it.

With one last sob. Shirley raised her head and gazed at Donovan. "I have no real choice, do I? I refuse to live with regrets. I would like to speak to your family and others, if I may. Then I can make the best decision for all of us."

Donovan handed two photos to Bill Roast and said, "One of these two women is the killer. I am sure of it."

Bill frowned. "Who are these people? Millicent Turner and Jean Mackey? I've never come across either one in my investigation." He stared at Donovan. "How did you come up with them?" He squinted at the photos. "And who took these photos? They're a bit fuzzy."

Donovan harrumphed. "They are clear enough to see that they both resemble the woman caught in those surveillance videos taken before and after some of the killings. They also look like the woman I remember from the second attempt on my life." He tapped on one of the photos. "This one, Millicent Turner, looks most familiar. I can't shake the feeling that I have met her somewhere, perhaps in a social setting. She's married to a lawyer. So that would make sense. The more prominent lawyers in Chicago pop up at all the high-profile social events."

"And the other?"

"Also the wife of an attorney. She is a bit more reclusive. We couldn't find out much about her. My bet is on Millicent Turner."

Bill shook his head. "Turner? That name hasn't come up in any of my investigations. I see no connection."

"Her professional name is Turner. Her husband's name is in the file. It's an odd one. Kissed? Or Quisp?"

Bill began searching through the file, throwing pages all over his desk. On the last page, he stopped to study it. A smile bloomed on his face. "No, it's Quist. Millicent Turner Quist. She's married to Dudley Horacio Quist, Esquire." He crowed, "Oh, we've got you now, baby. I can't wait until I plant your pretty, pampered little bottom in a cell."

Donovan cocked his head. "What I am missing? You're pretty confident she's the one. Don't you need to check her out? Check out her alibis? Right now, it's all circumstantial."

Bill scowled. "A car registered to Quist was sighted at the last murder. And even though we can't officially connect that murder to the others, I don't believe in coincidences." He gazed at Donovan. "How'd you get her name?"

"We have been playing with all sorts of lists, trying to find the common denominator between the victims. We narrowed it down to two strong possibilities. Matthew Donahue and Marshall Davis. So we ran background checks on both and sorted through their connections, families, spouses, things like that, looking for photos of anyone who resembled the perp. Those were the possibilities. Turner popped up on Donahue's side."

A puzzled expression crossed Bill's face. "What's the

connection? They don't share a surname."

"Matthew Donahue was married to Jillian Quist, Millicent's stepdaughter. He committed suicide two years ago. I counseled him through the Chicago Bar's mentorship program, but I thought we had an amicable relationship. I can't figure out what made me a target for murder."

"What about the judge?"

"All she's got is a resume on file, sent in for a clerkship. But she also knows Donahue through her legal fraternity. Neither seems a rational reason for murder. She rejects hundreds of applications each year. He was never even interviewed."

Bill's eyes narrowed. "You're right. That's a pretty weak reason for murder. It makes no sense. Serials are usually out for some sort of vengeance."

"And isn't it a little strange that a mother-in-law is out for blood? Why not the wife or the mother?"

Bill frowned. "I'll have to think about that, but you have to remember that nothing about murder is rational. This killer might be completely rational, a stone-cold killer. Or she may be some sort of crazy, loony toons. Any reason might be rational in her delusions. Anything on the other guy?"

"Jean Mackey is the birth mother of Marshall Davis. He was adopted as a baby. As far as we know, they have no relationship, which is why she's not at the top of the list. We know that Davis graduated from Northwestern. That means he had Professor Roberts for Contracts. All the first years do. He clerked his third year with Charles Wilson. Spent two years at Legal Services, but we haven't been able to confirm whether he and Garrett O'Shaunessy worked together. He was a part-time associate at Robert Melton's firm for a short time, then seems to have gone off the grid. Ultimately, he overdosed. Suspected suicide."

"What's the relationship to you and the judge?"

"That's where it gets confusing. As far as we can tell, he

attended one of my continuing legal education programs. Shirley thinks he has observed in her court."

"Kind of weak. Certainly not enough reason for two attempts on your life."

"That's what we thought, but all the other connections are more significant."

"Kid moved around a lot."

Donovan shrugged. "Sometimes, it takes a while to find the right fit. Ultimately, you may wind up deciding that you don't want to be a lawyer after all. Still, there's nothing in our records to warrant a killing spree. That's why we think Millicent Turner is a better bet." Donovan gazed at Bill. "So what's next?"

"I think it's time to interview Millicent Turner Quist." Bill held up a hand. "Let me rephrase that. I want *you* to interview her. Discovering that you're alive could trigger all sorts of reactions. When she sees your face, we'll know whether she's involved."

Bill didn't know that vampires were the ultimate diviners of truth. One look into the eyes of a human, and a vampire knew if they were speaking the truth. So a face-to-face wasn't a bad idea, just a little odd. Donovan ran a finger along the side of his nose. "Isn't that a little irregular, having an attorney in private practice conduct a police interrogation?"

Bill shook his head. "I'll sit in, but I'm betting she won't question it, whether or not she's guilty. Most have no real knowledge of what goes on in an investigation. There is no requirement that perps be questioned only by the police. We can invite anyone to the party."

"What if she lawyers up? Calls in her husband? He's no shrinking violet, you know. He's more like the commander of a tank regiment. He just rolls over everyone in front of him. Quist isn't the type to let anyone mess with his family, even if his wife proves to be a killer."

Bill chortled. "I'm counting on it. His reaction may tell us more than hers. Besides, after she sees you, we'll know instantly if she's involved by the expression on her face. We won't have to take it any further. I can take over."

Donovan's eyes narrowed. "So, you're using me as bait? Setting me up for a third attempt?"

Bill grinned. "Can you think of a better plan?"

The high society matron chuckled. Oh, it had been so much fun to watch that slut Millie Quist being led out of her home, that dumbfuck Dudley close behind, haranguing the police as if he was entitled to be treated differently than everyone else. She had hated Millie since the first day they met. All that innocence and guile. It was off-putting. Women like her set women's rights back centuries. She deserved to rot in jail. Even her husband acted like a fool around Millie. It would be nice to have her out of the way.

Too bad capital punishment had been abolished in Illinois. It would have been so much fun to watch Millie fry. Still, life in prison was nothing to sneeze at. After years and years confined to a cell, stripped of all her worldly pleasures, still decrying her innocence, Millie would become a mere shell of her former self. Empty and alone. As it should be.

She patted the blonde wig she wore. Chemo might have taken her hair, but it certainly hadn't sapped her thirst for revenge. It had taken her a while to put all the pieces together, and then cancer had created a delay, but once she had puzzled things out, everything fell into place. Her set-up was actually quite brilliant. The cops were completely confused. No one would suspect that she had engineered all those deaths from her ivory tower. After all, she was sick. But she hadn't missed a single detail.

The matron grinned. She had enjoyed these last few deaths

way too much. Too bad it had to end, eventually.

If only she could be a fly on the wall, to watch Millie sweat and squirm while she was interrogated by the police. If there was even a hint of guilt, she knew Dudley would do everything he could to avoid a messy, public trial. No, he would force her to take a plea, then divorce her before her side of the bed was cold. Dudley took his social standing quite seriously. He would not allow his reputation to be tainted by anyone or anything. He'd want the woman who was once his wife buried deep within the walls of a maximum-security prison. Then he would rewrite history and pretend she had never even existed. Find himself another trophy wife, and Millie would be forgotten.

The woman chuckled. She was by no means done, but she had already accomplished so much. Perhaps it was time for a break. Maybe she should take an extended stay at one of those spa islands. All of those cabana boys, so willing to please the guests. Yes, she would enjoy a young man's hands on her. Skillfully coaxing orgasms, causing her to tumble into unrelenting bliss. Just like in those romance novels everyone was so fond of. Nothing but sex, sun, sex, beach, sex, moonlight. How she would fly! Wouldn't that be fun?

She turned when she heard her husband shuffling down the hallway.

"They've taken Quist's wife in for questioning." He grunted. "Hard to imagine Millie a killer. She's just not the type."

The woman hid a smile. "I'm sure we can't know what people are capable of until they reach their breaking point." She shrugged. "Maybe poor Millie has reached hers."

# Chapter Sixteen: Not a Quist, a Twist

Donovan paced back and forth in the viewing room. Then he stopped and looked through the hidden mirror again. "She didn't do it, Bill. We've got the wrong woman. When she saw me, she didn't react at all. I don't think she even recognized me. Besides, she's smaller than the woman who confronted me at the courthouse, and although she wears a similar scent, it is different. It's not the same woman." Millie's eyes had been filled with terror. Not guilt. And her responses thus far were truthful, not a hint of a lie. He was almost disappointed. He had wanted, no needed, her to be the killer.

"You think she's being set up?"

"Possibly. Or maybe we're following the wrong clues. We're missing something. Something big." He turned to Molly. "Let me see Donahue's file again. I need to figure this out."

Molly handed the file to him. "I have an idea, boss. If you're sure it isn't her, show her the file. It's her son-in-law. Maybe she can help. Maybe they both can help. Maybe something they say will point to the real perp."

Bill nodded. "It's worth a try. I've got nothing to hold her on. She's more confused than anything. She was crying so much I thought she's was going to flood the room. She's not the cold, heartless killer I was expecting."

Molly gazed at Donovan. "Boss, can we talk a minute,

alone?"

Donovan nodded and led her out into the hallway.

Molly whispered, "You need to use The Lynx's report. There are enough sensory clues in there to nail the killer. It may not be Ms. Turner, but maybe she knows who fits those parameters."

Donovan frowned. "But how am I going to get that past Bill? He's going to wonder how I got that information."

"You're sneaky. Work it into general conversation. Tease it out of her."

Donovan sighed. "It's worth a shot. Remind me of the particulars."

"Guerlain cosmetics. A scent of Valmont hair products, but the scent was light. New user? Chanel tweed jacket, two thousand sixteen collection. Rust, apricot, gold, sage. Roja Haut Luxe Parfums."

Donovan's eyes narrowed. "Rather expensive tastes." He stroked his nose. "It seems contrary to Mrs. Quist. She does not seem like the extravagant type."

"Well, the car lead was a bust. Millicent's car was in the shop, so either the real killer borrowed it or the informant got the plate wrong. Still, I'm thinking the killer knows her. Maybe set her up."

Donovan nodded. "Why don't you divert Bill's attention for a few moments? Ask him to show you where the coffee is or something."

Molly smiled. "With pleasure."

Donovan grinned. Molly grabbed Bill's arms and led him away. Donovan said loudly, "I'll get started without you, wrap this up."

Bill turned back and shrugged. Molly tugged at his arm and they moved away.

When Bill was out of sight, he once again entered the interrogation room.

Dudley Quist scowled at him. "Now see here, Trait. Unless you have something on my wife, something you can use to hold her, I want her released."

Donovan smiled. "I just have a few more questions, Mrs. Quist. Then you'll be free to go. Let's return to your car. The two thousand eighteen BMW. Does anyone else drive your car?"

"No. There's only one set of keys. I keep them in my purse. My kids are out of the house and Dudley has his Porsche."

"What about passengers in recent weeks? Have you given anyone a ride, picked anyone up?"

Millicent frowned. "Well, I did pick up several women for lunch at the Country Club. You'd be amazed at the number of those women who don't drive. But I have been having a little trouble with my car. It's been running rough. The ladies kept telling me I needed it looked at. One even insisted I take it to a shop owned by someone from her church."

"And did you?"

Millicent blushed. "I did after it refused to start one morning. I had to have it towed."

"Towed where?"

"Louie's Car Works."

"Is that the place recommended to you?"

Millicent nodded. "When I called the auto club for assistance, they also recommended that garage."

"Who else knew your car was in the shop?"

Millicent shrugged. "Well, just Dudley. I did not need to tell anyone else."

Donovan sniffed the air. "By the way, that's a lovely scent you're wearing. Joy or Estee Lauder?"

Millicent stared at him. "Joy."

Donovan nodded. "A very attractive scent. It reminds me of a *parfum* I came across in Paris. Roget Luxera?"

Millicent giggled. "Oh, my. That's a little too pricey for me.

Unlike some of the others in my social circle, I stick to the perfume that suits me and I've never changed. I have been a Joy girl since college."

"Do you know anyone who does wear it?"

"Oh sure, Hillary James, Jean Mackey, a few others. Mostly the women who head to Paris and Milan for fashion week. I've never been particularly interested in that."

Dudley Quist smiled at his wife. "It's true. I had to force her to go through her closet and discard the older clothes she hoards. She had some suits that were so outdated, it was embarrassing."

She smiled at her husband fondly. "Well, no one will ever claim I'm fashion-forward. He's the clothes horse in the family. I'm a jeans-and-sweater girl."

Donovan studied the woman. "Discard them how? Do you donate them to a charity or a consignment shop? Or do you just throw them out?"

Millicent leaned forward, her eagerness to share apparent. "Actually, I donate them to a very special project. It basically provides clothing to women who are just entering or re-entering the workforce but lack the funds for appropriate clothing. Some of the clothing is sold, but most are distributed to women in need. I've been urging the women I know to do the same, since most of them clear out their closets annually, if not more often."

"Tell me about some of the clothing you donated."

Dudley laughed. "Everything she owned by Chanel, for one. I have been telling her those frumpy suits add twenty years at least. They may be popular among the moneyed set, but they are frightfully unattractive for a woman my wife's age. My word, she's in her forties, not her sixties."

Donovan nodded. "One last question. Have you ever heard of Classique hair care products?"

Millicent scrunched her nose. "I think so. Isn't that the one women use to thicken their hair? It's also for women who lose their hair, through chemo and other medical procedures. That's really expensive and requires a prescription." Millicent tossed her thick, shoulder-length blonde hair off a shoulder. "I have no need for it. I buy my hair products off the drugstore shelf. My hair has always been full-bodied. I've never really invested a lot of money on it."

Donovan smiled at her. "Mrs. Quist, thank you for your time. You are free to go." He opened the door to the interview room and ushered them out.

Bill walked up and watched the Quists leave. "Now what? She was the best lead we had."

"Not necessarily. She gave me some names, some other possibilities. While Molly checks them out, I think we need to shake things up. I think it's time that Donovan Trait returns from the dead." Donovan smirked. "Well, almost dead."

Donovan leaned over and bussed Shirley's cheek. "No need to be so nervous, my dear. Our intended killer doesn't know we survived. Save the worry and fears for our next public outing." He moved Shirley down the red carpet to a waiting entertainment reporter. "Smile for the cameras, dear."

Cameras flashed and paparazzi shouted as Donovan and Shirley approached. He blinked at all the lights trained on him. While it was unnatural light, it was still a bit unsettling. He turned from it and smiled at the waiting reporter. "Hello, Gina," he said, forcing himself to be friendly. When not on camera, Gina James was a barracuda. If she wanted a man, she sank her teeth in and didn't let go. His one date with the woman had been a disaster.

"Well, Donovan Trait," she exclaimed brightly. "I see that rumors of your death were a bit premature. Thousands of women in Chicagoland were on pins and needles during your latest ordeal. We did not take your potential demise lightly."

She squeezed his arm and pulled him in for a peck on his cheek. "I am so glad to see you have recovered."

Donovan turned on the charm. "Well, thank you, Gina. It's good to be back. My recovery was a bit arduous, but I was determined." He pulled Shirley next to him. "Determined to return to my lady love." He gazed into Shirley's eyes. "Of course, then she was attacked, and she had to fight her way back to me."

Dawn blinked. "Oh yes, you're Judge . . . Marilyn Magnus? Right, also an intended victim of The Butcher."

Donovan's eyes widened in surprise. "The what?"

Gwen waved him off. "Just something we call him around the newsroom. Dick the Butcher is the Shakespeare character who delivers that line, *The first thing we do, let's kill all the lawyers*. Isn't that the message the killer has been leaving with the bodies?"

Donovan frowned. That little tidbit had not been released to the media or the public. Now the media was going to have a field day with it. Keeping his voice calm, Donovan replied, "Unfortunately, I was too busy recuperating to know the details of the police investigation. I can neither confirm nor deny their findings. However, speculation is rampant. I would caution you to verify your facts. We don't want even more scurrilous details to be bandied about. The only person that benefits is the killer."

Gina blanched. "I didn't mean . . ." She quickly pivoted to Shirley. "Judge Magnus, how lucky are you to be on the arm of one of Chicago's hottest lawyers?"

Before Shirley could respond, Donovan gently guided the mic back to him. "On the contrary, it is I who is lucky. I want the world to know that I am in love with Judge *Shirley Magnusen* and I intend to do everything possible to convince her to be my bride."

Gina gasped. "Oh, my. Does that mean Donovan Trait is

off the market?"

Donovan smiled at Shirley and kissed her passionately. He held her tightly to him as he gazed directly into the camera, a triumphant smile on his face. "Most definitely. I have found the woman with whom I wish to live out my remaining years."

"Sorry, ladies," Shirley said with a smile. She grabbed Donovan's arm. "This one is taken." She gazed up into Donovan's eyes and winked. "He's mine."

Gina's gaze swept Shirley's body from head to toe and apparently found her lacking. She scowled into the camera, "Well, that's a real surprise. But you heard it here first, folks, Donovan Trait is in love."

Donovan smiled and moved Shirley to the next reporter. "Sorry about that," he murmured.

Shirley giggled. "Up until you declared your love, I thought she was going to dive into your pants."

He tugged on her hand. "Come on. We need to share the news with the rest of the media. I don't want Gina to think she's got an exclusive."

Shirley snuggled into him. "I've noticed something this evening, darling."

"What's that?"

"People are genuinely delighted to see you. Sure, you're the epitome of charm, and you're gorgeous, but people genuinely like you. They are glad you survived the attack. That says a lot about you. When we first met, I couldn't see past the façade. I thought the consummate gentleman thing was all an act. But it isn't. You are everything you appear to be. I'm impressed."

Donovan smiled. He buried his face in her blonde curls and crooned, "Enough to marry me?"

Shirley grinned. She took both of his hands into hers and gazed up into his eyes. "I believe so. We'll work out the rest."

Donovan whooped and everyone in the crowd turned toward him. He grabbed Shirley in his arms and swung her around. Then he put her down and yelled, "She said, *yes*!"

The applause was loud, almost deafening, as people joined in the celebration.

Donovan dropped to one knee and reached into the pocket of his tuxedo. He pulled out a box from an exclusive jeweler and slipped an elegant ring comprised of rose gold, diamonds, and rubies onto her finger. "I've been carrying this around for weeks, just waiting for you to say *yes*."

A single tear dripped from Shirley's eye. "How could I say, no? You're my person. The only person I'll ever need."

Donovan stood and pulled her into a hug. He chuckled. "Do you really want to see this opera, or shall we head home, for other entertainment?"

"Well, *La Boheme* is one of my favorites. The story is filled with such passion. Truth be told, I get swept away by Mimi, the seamstress. In my fantasies . . ." She blushed. "But I have seen it countless times. I would much rather spend my evening cuddled up next to you . . . my future husband."

Donovan grinned. "Well, then. Let's enter the building and exit through a stage door. No one will be the wiser."

As he stepped toward the entrance of the Lyric Opera House, Shirley pulled on his arm. "Wait," she whispered. "We need our bodyguards to catch up. The killer could be anywhere."

Donovan frowned. Their appearance was intended to alert the killer that they had survived. He did not expect her to make an attempt tonight. However, the killer had surprised them before. She probably wouldn't think twice about pulling out her handgun and shooting them in a dark, crowded theatre. It could be the perfect crime. With the lights down low, the audience's attention focused on the stage, and all the music and sound effects, a gunshot or knife would barely be noticed. Until the curtain closed and the lights went up, the dead would go undiscovered.

However, their attendance at this fundraiser has been unannounced. It was intended to make a splash in the media. The police had investigated every name the Quists had produced, and had everyone, including the Quists, under surveillance. Bill seemed convinced that the killer wouldn't have time to make a kill this evening.

Donovan hoped he was right. He placed his arm around Shirley and pulled her closer to him. In the end, this was about the risk to Shirley, not himself. He could survive almost anything. As a human, Shirley could not.

He smiled at the woman he loved and nuzzled her neck. "Let's go home. My fangs are getting itchy."

# Chapter Seventeen: A Sibling's Desires

Judge Marilyn Trait was enraged.

It was bad enough her brother had come out of hiding, presenting himself as a target for every gun-happy harpy in Chicagoland. By miraculously rising from the near-dead, he had effectively blunted her newfound power on the Vampire Coalition.

No longer would she be allowed to champion her causes. The Coalition would sweep her aside and insist on Donovan's presence. Her father didn't care. He already held a board position. Holding Donovan's proxy was just gravy. She, however, had bigger plans. Not quite a coup, but a challenge to authority. She could not possibly gain their attention on the rights of the female vampires unless she had a seat at the table. Now that was about to disappear.

Marilyn tapped her fingers on her desk. Maybe she could appeal to his new love, the Honorable Shirley Magnusen. She was a human and unaware of the governance structure of the vampire kingdom, but surely she had some interest in empowering women. She was a judge, after all. Although the judiciary had made great strides over the years, it was still a bit sexist, if not misogynist. Many of the older judges had gone to law school when women were a rarity. They couldn't fathom why a woman would want a career, much less practice law. To the older male judges, it was unseemly.

She expelled a frustrated sigh. The judiciary had nothing

on a coalition of centuries-old vampires. For them, the good old days referred to the seventeenth and eighteenth centuries where women were enslaved by tradition and propriety. Marilyn snorted. In those days, if a man even looked at you the wrong way, you were expected to marry him. So she had stuck her head in her law books and ignored the male population. In her mind, marriage was a trap to be avoided at all costs.

It wasn't until the nineteen sixties that she had finally been able to breathe. It wasn't just burning her bra, it was also the sudden entitlement to make her own choices. Marilyn had dumped the girdle and embraced every aspect of sexual freedom. Her family had raised their eyebrows but said nothing as she feasted and experimented and climaxed with abandon. Most of it was done with humans, of course. They weren't seeking a relationship. They just wanted to have fun. The vampire nation had been appalled, but female vamps of a certain age had felt reborn.

Unfortunately, the gains made during those years had been whittled away. One step forward, three steps back. Human females were waking up to that fact and they were making their voices heard. However, female vamps were at risk of offending the Coalition. If they approached the issues the wrong way, they risked social exile. When you were a vampire, exclusion was much worse than any other punishment the Coalition could mete out.

Still, the Coalition's refusal to address the rights of female vamps was a festering sore. It needed to be resolved. Women vamps needed true representation on the Coalition. A voice in proposed breeding initiatives. A ban against arranged and sometimes coerced marriages. And the all too human maladies, such as domestic violence, gender discrimination, and reproduction rights. Mixed marriages—unions between humans or weres—were still frowned upon. While a male vampire was permitted a human mate of his choosing—if the mate agreed to be turned—female vamps were forbidden from marrying anyone outside their species. Period. No explanation whatsoever. It wasn't fair. It wasn't right.

Marilyn began to doodle on her legal pad. She had been lucky. When she began to chafe at all the restrictions, her parents had granted her access to the human world. Unlike many of her friends, she had been allowed to explore. When she had fallen in love with a human the first time, her father had merely said, "That simply isn't appropriate among our kind." The second time, her mother had comforted her and said, "Dear one, why would you choose to be enslaved to a human who will eventually die before you and leave you all alone?" The third time, Marilyn had kept her mouth shut and after persistent marriage proposals, tearfully walked away. Since then, she had toyed with humans, but she now kept her heart locked permanently shut. It just wasn't worth the pain.

Her mother danced into her chambers, her face alight with joy. She clapped her hands with excitement. "Did you hear, my darling? Donovan has proposed to Shirley and she said *yes*! Oh, isn't it wonderful? After all these years, to finally find his soulmate? The mother of his children? The yin to his yang? It reminds me of the first time I saw your father. It was love at first sight. I simply couldn't imagine loving anyone else."

Marilyn scowled. "Mother, it was an arranged marriage. Love had nothing to do with it. You told me after you met Father, you ran and hid in the gardens."

Gwendolyn Trait laughed. "Oh, I was such a silly girl back then. It was much later that I recognized the magic of that night. I had no doubt your Father was the one."

Marilyn snorted. "Mother, please. Sit down. You're hallucinating."

Her mother plopped into an armchair and gently rearranged the pleats on her skirts. "Stop being so negative,

Lynnie. Your time will come."

"What the hell are you talking about?"

"Don't you see? Donovan has found a human who loves him as he is. She accepts his dominant genes. She adores his recessive ones. One day she will bear little vamps. I'll finally become a Nana. After all of these years, we'll have the pitter-patter of little ones racing through our house."

"Mother, you already have the pitter-patter of little feet. You have dogs and cats."

"Oh, why must you be so unpleasant? If everything works out, I'm sure you'll be the next in line."

Marilyn sighed. On a good day, a conversation with *La Mere* was taxing. "In line for what? Marriage? That would require finding a suitable groom. And the kind of man who attracts me would be too much of an Alpha to compromise. Besides, no human wants a woman with a barren womb. Not when so many human females could bear him a normal child."

Her mother pursed her lips. "How do you know until you've tried? There are so many options now. If Donovan is willing to try, why aren't you?"

Marilyn scowled. "Because every time I have fallen in love, you and Father put an end to it."

Her mother waved her off. "Oh, that. You were such a child back then. Too enamored with being in love and easy sex. You're older now. More mature. Now you can attract the right kind of man. Someone who can love you for the amazing woman you are."

Marilyn blinked. Then she stared at her mother. Ye Gods, the woman almost looked sincere. She frowned. What if she *was* sincere? Marilyn tried to squelch the odd feeling that filled her heart. Humans called it *hope*.

Gwendolyn Trait gazed at her and a sly smile crossed her face. "There are a lot of fish in the sea, darling. Time to cast your line and reel one in, vamp, were, or human."

The matron scowled at the Tribune. Donovan Trait was alive. Dammit, what kind of man survived two murder attempts? Surely, the man wasn't human. And the judge was alive and well, too. She had packed enough C4 under the secretary's desk to take out the entire floor. How had the judge survived?

The matron slapped the paper down on the dining room table. She scratched the fuzz that was growing back on her scalp. The woman sneered. Her little guppy had ended his life way before his time. It wasn't right that Trait and his lady love continued to live and celebrate. There would be no marriage. She would see to that.

Wearily, she reached for her cup of tea. Dammit, she was exhausted. Between the second round of chemo and radiation, and the cancer eating away at her brain, she was tuckered out by day's end. Killing was almost . . . well . . . killing her. She laughed bitterly. Everything else just added to the stress. She didn't know if she would survive, but she did know that as long as she could function, she would avenge her little guppy's death. Anyone who had read his journal would have done the same.

No one deserved such humiliation. The utter devastation of failing again and again so publicly. That was why every person on her list deserved to die. They had played a role in his humiliation. They had permitted it to happen. Not one of them had fought for her poor guppy. They had stood back and watched while he flailed in the shark pond.

Watching Millie Quist being hauled off in handcuffs had been a delight. The police had followed the clues she left like hungry little mice after their last bite of cheese. She had found Millie's jacket at the consignment shop where she volunteered and planted it at the site of Robert Melton's death. She had called in the sighting of Millie's car near O'Shaunessy's house, using a prepaid cell phone, just in case someone called back to verify. No one ever did. Fools.

She sipped her tea. It was a shame they had let Millie go. It had been a perfect set up.

She smiled. They would never find her. They simply lacked the intelligence. They would need to find her guppy's diary to find the link, and she had buried the diary with him, after reading it of course. She had paid the funeral director to place the diary in her guppy's casket right before it had been sealed. No one had seen the transaction, and unless questioned, the funeral director was unlikely to remember. Besides, people buried things with the dead all the time. It wasn't like she was breaking the law or anything.

The matron yawned. She was dreaming of her poor guppy more often now. It was as if he was calling to her, holding his arms out in a welcome embrace.

The doctors couldn't tell her whether she was going to live or die. One week, the tumor looked like it was shrinking, the next week it was enlarged. All she knew was that when she did depart this Earth, her poor guppy would be waiting. Fully avenged.

Donovan peered over the top of the Tribune and watched Shirley peruse the society pages. She was giggling. Finally, he asked, "What's so funny?

"I think you dashed the hopes and dreams of most of the women at that fundraiser." She held up a page with a photo of him proposing. "Look at the expression on those women's faces. In the background. Some of them look positively crestfallen. And the headline is hysterical, *Donovan Trait struck by cupid's arrow*. I never truly realized what a catch you are, darling."

Donovan waggled his brows. "Ye Gods, woman. I'm one of Chicagoland's most wanted, and not for any criminal acts."

Shirley guffawed. She started giggling again, holding her stomach. "I'm sorry," she sputtered. "It's just too . . . too much to take in. They treat you like you're male perfection, and you're not even human. What does that say about human males?"

Donovan grinned. "That vampire males are superior?" He chuckled. "In every single way."

"Oh my God, I can't stand it." Shirley giggled so hard tears began to run down her face. "The joke is on them, and I can't even tell anyone. How do you stand it? How can you watch all the peacocks in the legal profession strutting their stuff when they can't even begin to . . ." She waved a hand at his nether region. "As if they could even compare . . ."

Donovan gazed at Shirley, his amusement causing his mouth to form into a wicked grin. "So it's all about my family jewels, is it? I feel so cheap."

Shirley's giggles stopped abruptly and an expression of horror crossed her face. "Oh darling, I didn't mean to objectify you. I would never do that. It's just that people are so shallow. Here you are, a brilliant lawyer, and no one can see past your good looks and er . . . *family jewels*. It's so human. How did you even stand it? Don't you find it offensive?"

Donovan rolled his eyes. "Please, I've had centuries of women throwing themselves at me, trying to get beneath the cloak, so to speak. That's why it took me so long to find true love. You love me for me. You see all of me."

Shirley smirked. "Still, your skill in all areas is rather superior. I can't believe I'm so lucky. You truly are the total package for a human female, and you're not even human." Another giggle bubbled up. "The irony is killing me."

"I don't think anyone else has ever found so much merriment in the fact that I am a vampire, darling."

Shirley reached for her cup of coffee and took a long sip. As she drank, she tried to hold her smile at bay. "Look, I don't know what's going to happen here—whether I will go through the turning or not. The female vampires I've spoken with have been helpful, but I'm still not there. I just know whatever we decide, *whenever* we decide, I am going to enjoy every single minute of my life with you." She stood and settled onto Donovan's lap, grabbing his head and kissing him hard. "Mine," she purred. "You're all mine."

"Ahem."

Donovan turned and scowled. "Later, Bryce. Can't you see we're busy here?"

Bryce chortled. "Oh, it's plain you're up to *something*, but your friend, the detective is on his way in. He didn't want to interrupt, so he went for a drive around the block. You made him blush. All that cooing and oohing. It's worse than watching porn. You two are disgusting." He gestured toward Shirley and the satin peignoir set she wore. "May I suggest that Judge Magnusen change into something less . . . I mean *more* suitable for company?"

Shirley gazed at her skimpy nightgown and her face reddened. She jumped to her feet. "Yes, of course," she sputtered. "I wasn't expecting company." She quickly left the room.

"Dammit, Bryce, things were just getting interesting."

Bryce cocked an eyebrow. "I imagine you have plenty of time for *that*. Centuries and centuries, in fact. Now, may I show the good detective in?"

Donovan emitted a long sigh. "Ye Gods, it isn't even nine. That man visits at the worst possible times."

'He's your friend, not mine. Next time, tell him you don't entertain visitors until noon."

Donovan waved him off. "Oh, show him in. Might as well see what he wants, not that I have anything better to do."

Bryce nodded and a minute later, returned with Bill.

Bill grinned. "I told you to be seen, man. I didn't tell you to get engaged. Even the wife was pouting this morning. You've broken a lot of hearts."

"Oh well, it had to happen sometime. Maybe all those heartbroken women will move on to someone else."

"Or just try harder. Some women won't care if you're taken, though I imagine they might be intimidated by the judge. She looks like she could unleash some rather sharp claws."

*Or fangs.* Donovan smiled at the thought. "Shirley knows she has absolutely no worries there. I am a faithful, monogamous man. Truly in love, with no intention of straying." *It's not like I'm human.*

Bill gazed at him. "Huh? Who would have thunk? You dropped that playboy façade faster than dirty underwear. I didn't know you had it in you."

Donovan shrugged. "People see what they want to see. Believe what they need to believe. It's not my fault they lack imagination."

Bill plopped into a chair at the dining table, picked up a pastry, and took a bite. "So, you're really going to go for it?"

Donovan nodded. "Absolutely."

"Well, I was going to congratulate you on a great performance last night, but obviously there was no acting involved. Still, the deal's not sealed until you get the judge down the aisle. Who knows, she may change her mind."

"Not likely, Detective." Shirley walked into the room, now dressed in an elegant blue silk sheath. "We'll both be pledging our troths at that alter, no doubts, no qualms." She settled at the dining table and gazed at Bill. "What brings you here at such an early hour?"

Bill set down his pastry and brushed his lips with his hand. "We might have a break in the case. We have been backtracking through Donahue and Davis' lives, starting with their deaths. The funeral director for the Davis funeral had a rather strange recollection. Before the burial, but after the casket was sealed, some woman wanted him to stick a journal inside the casket. He tried to tell her the casket was sealed, that he couldn't reopen it without family or court approval, but she got very angry and started threatening him. Finally, she offered him money. To prevent a scene, he just took the book and promised to put it in the casket."

"What did he do with the journal?" Shirley asked. "Did he toss it?"

Bill shook his head. "No, he stuck it in a drawer. Said they were practically on the way to the cemetery. He had no time to do anything with it."

Donovan's eyes narrowed, "So where is it? Is it Davis' diary or someone else's?"

"Not sure. Check your email. I had one of my techs scan it into a document. Your names are in it. But I can't tell if the writer was in love with *youse* or hated *youse*. The commentary makes no sense to me."

Shirley held up her hands. "That's not as strange as you might think. Even judges have their groupies. People who hang out in the courtroom to watch us work. We call them *bench ho's*. And they don't discriminate based on gender." She frowned. "Though I think it's more about fan worship than lust. Heck, even some of the older judges have people who sit in on every trial. Some of the people get a bit stalkerish and have to be removed. Still, that's not a reason to kill anyone, at least a group of lawyers. That's just delusional."

Bill stared at her. "Did you think the killer was sane? They *are* delusional."

Shirley shrugged. "Point taken. Still, there has to be something more. The spurned fan might fly for Donovan, but not for me. I don't recall ever having someone repeatedly sit in on my trials. People leave *him* gifts."

Donovan blushed. "All returned, when possible, I assure

you. I never know if the gifts are a symbol of adoration or a bribe." He shuddered. "Either way, it's just inappropriate."

Bill snorted. "Well, all I know is the journal has your names in it. I need you to take a gander and see if it makes any sense to you. But we're focusing more heavily on Davis now. So I need you to think hard about any contact you had with him." He nodded at Donovan. "I sent you the scan. Take a look."

Donovan began to scroll through his phone. "I'll send a copy to Shirley and we'll go through it together."

Shirley nodded. "Maybe the answer is staring us in the face. Do we know who provided the journal to the funeral director?"

Bill sighed. "All the funeral director remembered was that she was middle-aged and very pushy. And wealthy. He said she was dressed to the nines."

Shirley made a face. "So, we're back to square one?"

Bill toyed with his now half-eaten pastry. "Maybe not. Read the journal. Maybe you'll catch more than I did." He pushed the pastry away and stood. "I went through it quickly. I need to go through it again. Let's chat once you've finished your copies."

Donovan nodded. "We'll get right on it. After our miraculous recovery was exposed last night, we're officially taking the week off. We need to reacclimate to life among the living."

Bill chortled. "Well, stay out of the way of the killer, wouldja?" He wandered out of the library.

Donovan smiled at Shirley. "I'll ask Bryce to brew up some more tea and that cinnamon hazelnut coffee you so love. We've got hours of reading ahead."

# Chapter Eighteen: A Killer Defanged?

Donovan put down his reader and frowned. "I don't get it. This journal sounds like the rantings of a very disturbed person. For the life of me, I can't fathom how either of the men we identified factor in."

Shirley closed her laptop and sighed. "None of this has made sense, darling. We aren't dealing with a stable mind. It's like the killer picked her victims, not for anything they've done, but simply for the fact that they were named by someone else. All I got out of it was that someone resented me for my appearance. According to this, I am guilty of nothing that warrants my death."

Donovan slowly stirred his tea. "Still, I think Bill is right. This sounds more like it was written by a woman, not a man."

Shirley entwined her fingers, lost in thought. Finally, she said, "What if these are the musings of a woman in a man's body? What if this is more about how society views gender issues than anything else? The legal profession is pretty conservative. I imagine a lawyer considering a gender change would feel shunned, even afraid. It might boil down to a choice between career or personal happiness. That's not a decision that is easy to make."

"Especially if you're already married with a child. A man might feel good *and* trapped." Donovan ran a hand through his dark hair. "Still, in all my conversations with Donahue, I never once got the impression he was uncomfortable with his gender. In fact, it was the opposite. He seemed very much a man. And I didn't have enough contact with Davis to get an impression either way."

"Well, if this is about Davis, we may never know."

Donovan absently toyed with his reader. "We seem to have a whole lot of nothing. I can't make head or tails of this journal. I see no reason to attack any of the attorneys listed. I really think it's a dead end."

Shirley shut down her laptop and gazed at Donovan. "Unless it means something to the writer. So, what do we do now? Wait around like hapless fools until she strikes again?"

Donovan expelled a long breath. "I hate to say it, but we need to find a way to draw her out. To force her to act. That's the only way to catch her."

Shirley groaned. "You want to act as bait, again? Is that really a good idea? What if she succeeds in killing one of us, but not the other? I'm the one most likely to die. I'm not a vampire. For you, there is almost no risk."

Donovan gazed at her. If nothing else, this situation made a forceful argument for being turned. Sure, it would take a while, but once the process began, Shirley's chances of survival increased exponentially. "Given the circumstances, maybe it's best if I am the bait. We can keep you sequestered here. Then the only real risk is that I may wind up temporarily incapacitated."

Shirley's eyes filled. "Dammit, I hate being the weak link." She tugged at a blonde curl. "Maybe it's time I [illegible]." She reached for Donovan's hand. "I, you know . . . was turned."

Donovan studied her. "Are you sure? This is forever. Once you start, there's no going back."

Shirley hesitated. "I won't be responsible for any harm that comes to you, and if I am killed, you told me your heart will break. And that could kill *you*. There is no way I want that hanging over me. It seems like there is no choice. If I want a life with you, and I *do*, I have to take this risk." Her eyes glistened. "I've spoken to enough turned women to know what to expect. I know what precautions to take. But it's time to stop pussyfooting around. Either I take this leap of faith or I walk away. I couldn't bear the alternative."

She held up a hand. "However, I do want children. One of the women I spoke with suggested I harvest my eggs before turning and freeze them. When we are ready to have children, we can figure out the rest. I may not be able to carry our children, but in all other respects, I will be their mother. I'm not sure if that will meet with your Coalition's approval, but maybe someday."

Donovan stood. "Okay, I'll make the call. We'll do it here. The process can be a bit exhausting, physically, and emotionally. I want to be the one who guides you through this."

Shirley gave him a slight smile. "I wouldn't have it any other way." Her expression became stern. "And Donovan, don't you dare put yourself out there as bait. Not until we can take on this monster together."

The high society matron lay in bed. Her body couldn't seem to decide whether it wanted to be hot or cold. One moment she was sweating, then she was as cold as ice. What the heck was going on? It had been weeks since her last treatment. She had never gotten this sick before. She couldn't eat, she couldn't sleep, she couldn't function.

Dammit. This was not supposed to happen. She was supposed to get well. She was supposed to be getting stronger. Then why did she feel so weak? It was almost as if the cancer had come back. Panic filled her. No, that couldn't be it. She was just stressed out because Trait and that judge has messed up her mission. She had to figure out how to make sure they died before she did.

She sat up in bed and quickly slid back down, resting her head on her pillow. Dammit, she felt ill. It was overpowering. How was she supposed to execute her targets when she couldn't even sit up, much less stand? Of one thing she was certain. She could not give up. She owed it to her little guppy. For all of the wrongs he had suffered. If she didn't take a stand, no one else would.

She managed to sit up. Then she carefully moved her legs to the floor. If she just moved slowly, she could get out the door.

She pushed herself off the bed and landed on her feet. She struggled to get her balance. Her stomach tumbled and churned. She felt so sick. As the bile began to build, she grabbed a nearby vase and unloaded the contents of her stomach. The matron took an uncertain step and the vase crashed to the floor. She wavered for a moment and whimpered, confused. Her mind began to fog and her legs became water. She fought the darkness as she slid to the floor.

Her last thought was, "I'm not done . . ."

Shirley frowned as Donovan stood up from the desk chair and began to pace.

Then Bill stood up from his armchair and followed.

Both muttered as they did so. Occasionally, one would stop and glare at the other, but mostly there was no conversation. No expletives. Just nonsensical muttering.

Finally, Shirley threw down the report she had been reading and stalked toward the two men. She stood between them and held out her arms. "Just stop it, you two. You're behaving like children. Spoiled brats, to be fair. Why are you reacting so childishly to something out of your control? It's not like you failed."

Donovan snarled, "But we won't get justice, either. I have

a right to face my executioner and demand justice." He pointed at her with a dramatic swish of his arm. "And so do you."

Shirley shook her head. "Dammit, Donovan. You don't always get what you want in this life." She grabbed his hand and nudged him toward his chair. "Now sit, or there will be consequences."

Bill snickered. "Going to make him sleep on the sofa?" He grinned. "This place has twelve bedrooms. He never has to sleep on the sofa . . ."

She turned to Bill and made a zipping motion across her mouth, then perched her hands on her hips and shot him a stink eye. "And you, Bill. You're a cop. You know better. This is the first time Donovan has been targeted by a killer. Of course he wants revenge. He can be excused for acting irrationally. You, on the other hand, have thirty years on the force, during which you have put hundreds of criminals away. You know there's always a fifty percent chance you won't get justice. The risk of something going wrong is always there. Witnesses recant. Evidence gets lost. The accused dies. The course of justice does not always run smoothly. So just zip it."

A look of chagrin crossed Bill's face. He returned to his chair and with a dramatic sigh, sunk onto the cushion. "Yeah, but this is the first time the killer went off on people I knew. People I actually like. Friends. I never wanted someone brought to justice more."

Shirley's mouth curled slightly at the edges. She gazed at Donovan, then at Bill. "Look, you figured out who the killer is. It's not your fault you can't take her into custody. For God's sake, she's been taken to Switzerland, in a coma no less, as a last-ditch effort to save her life."

Bill frowned. "And if she survives, do you think she'll return to Chicago to face the music? Of course not. She has money up the *wazoo*. She could happily live out her years on some remote island, free and clear. Never having to pay for what she's done."

"At least we know the reason she went after us," Shirley said. "Marshall Davis was the son she gave up for adoption when she was in her twenties. He was the child she watched from afar. She misinterpreted a lot of things that occurred in his life, blaming people not deserving of blame, and when he killed himself, she just blew. Obviously, Jean Mackey needs to be brought to justice if at all possible." Shirley took a deep breath. "But right now, she has something like a five percent chance of survival. That means she has a ninety-five percent chance of dying. If she survives, you have all of your ducks in a row. A grand jury indictment. An arrest warrant. A certified extradition request. The Swiss have even taken the extraordinary step of arresting her and placing her under armed guard, even though she's in a coma."

"You think so, huh?" Bill scowled. "There's something fishy about this. Why go to all that expense for something that the docs say only has a five percent chance of working? It wasn't to cure her. It was to get her out of the country. And the only reason to get out of the country was to avoid prosecution. Why? If she's going to die anyway, *why*?" He shook his head slowly. "For all we know, her docs could have been paid to lie about her condition. We were never able to verify her condition before she was gone. Crap, I would feel so much better if we could have served the arrest warrant, coma or not."

Donovan entwined his fingers, his expression thoughtful. "It's as if an arrest for murder in America would exclude her from something . . ."

Shirley's eyes widened. "Or maybe exclude her husband from something, like an inheritance. She's in a coma. He isn't."

Bill sat up in his chair. "You mean like some sort of wrongful acts exclusion in a will or trust? I've heard of those. They're usually in one of those fancy Dynasty Trusts. You know, the ones that pass billions from generation to generation, creating a class of the idle rich? I read about it in one of those business magazines." He paused and screwed up his face in thought.

Donovan stared off into space, then his eyes slowly narrowed. "What if they plan to fake her death, but he needs a clean slate to collect any inheritance? Being charged with a crime is not tantamount to a conviction. In this country, you are innocent until proven guilty. Usually, a *wrongful acts exclusion* requires a conviction."

Shirley nodded. "That could apply to so many things, not just inheritance. A payout from an income trust or voting rights in a partnership or corporation."

"Dammitall," Bill bellowed. "I knew it. Some way, somehow, this is going to bite me in the behind."

# Chapter Nineteen: Judgement

Shirley nervously pulled at the sleeve of her deep blue business suit.

She hadn't been this nervous since taking the state bar exam. She was sure she was going to vomit.

Donovan squeezed her hand, his expression sympathetic. "Relax, darling. They won't bite." He smirked. "Maybe I should rephrase that . . ."

Shirley curled into him. "I think being forced to sign a non-disclosure agreement that listed death as the penalty for its violation has left me a bag of nerves. I know I can do this. I *have* to do it. Without their approval, I lose the one thing that matters more than anything else." She reached up and stroked his face. "You."

The tall, ornate wooden doors opened and a solemn man, dressed all in black, beckoned.

To human eyes, he would be perfectly ordinary, but Shirley knew he was not. He was a vampire.

The man's eyes appeared to take her measure, then he scowled and turned away.

Shirley felt as if her heart had dropped onto the floor. "Oh, my," she whispered. "That can't be good at all."

Donovan brushed a quick kiss across her lips. "No worries, darling. This is a mere formality. Old Jeffers may not approve of humans, but he only has one-seventh of the vote. We need four votes for approval, and my father and I hold two of those. We've got this."

Donovan ushered Shirley into a cavernous room. The walls

were sculpted wood, each carved with intricate scenes. Shirley removed her arm from Donovan's and began to walk around the room, studying each. Some were beautiful, some were horrific, and some were just plain strange. She got the sense that the panels were intended to convey history, but without further explanation, they were more confusing than informative.

At the front of the room sat a long wooden table with six men seated behind it. They all sat quietly, but Shirley could feel their eyes on her. Inwardly, she gulped. Someone cleared their throat.

Donovan walked to her and took her arm. "Time to face the music," he said. He escorted her to one of two chairs sitting before the panel.

When they were seated, Shirley studied the group. Six men of all ages, shapes, sizes, and races sat quietly. Her focus moved to the seventh chair. It was empty. Shirley leaned toward Donovan. "Shouldn't you be sitting up there?"

"Not in this case. My vote has already been decided. And nothing I say will change my mind." He grinned at her.

Shirley bit back a giggle.

The man seated in the center of the table rose. "Donovan Jonathon Trait, the Coalition of the Vampire Kingdom has assembled at your request. All matters discussed forthwith shall remain within this room, revealed to no one, upon penalty of death." The man's gaze moved to Shirley and she shivered. "You have brought a human to this court. Do you assume full responsibility for her words and actions? Will you accept any penalties mandated by her conduct?"

Donovan stood. "I will accept any and all penalties you choose to assess, My Lord."

The man nodded. "Do you attest to her veracity? The truthfulness of her heart, mind, and soul?"

Donovan nodded. "I do, My Lord."

The man nodded. "You may proceed."

Donovan took Shirley's hand and gently helped her to her feet. "My Lords, I would like to introduce you to Judge Shirley Agnes Magnusen." He took her hand. "You have all received and had time to review my petition to grant an exception to Rule Fourteen Hundred Point Two, Miscegenation. Intermarriage between breeds and races. After more than three hundred years, more than one hundred and fifty of which I have served on this Coalition, I have found myself in love with a human. She has accepted my proposal of marriage and it is my greatest desire to receive the blessing of this council."

Another vampire, one with darker skin and gray, grizzled hair, asked, "And if you do not receive that blessing?"

Shirley stiffened, trying to control her fear.

Donovan squeezed her hand and smiled at her. Then he lifted his eyes to gaze at the man who had posed the question. "Then I am afraid I will be forced to resign from this Coalition and accept exile from the Vampire Empire, My Lord.

Shirley bit back a gasp. Donovan was willing to leave his world for hers? No, that wasn't what she wanted. She hadn't even asked. Shirley started to speak, but Donovan again squeezed her hand, and she bit her lip.

"I see," observed another vampire.

Shirley's attention moved to that man. He appeared much younger than the previous speaker. Mid-fifties, pleasantly handsome. A sincere smile.

"Has there been a discussion about a forced turning?" the man asked.

"Yes, My Lord," Donovan responded. "We have discussed it at length."

The man gazed at Shirley. "And what has been decided, in her words, please."

Shirley took a deep breath. Softly, she said, "I have spoken with other women who have undergone the forced turning, My Lord, and I have concluded that while the process seems challenging, it is not unbearable. I have given my consent."

The man cocked an eyebrow. "I see. No fear of the unknown? No regrets about leaving your human life behind?"

Shirley allowed herself a slight smile. "I would be foolish not to be afraid, My Lord. I would be even more foolish not to fear leaving the human world." She gazed at Donovan. "But I love this man and I want to be with him for the rest of my days. He can't be turned into a human, so the only answer is for me to join the vampire world. Marriage is about compromise. This is a compromise I make knowingly and willingly . . . and lovingly. No one will ever doubt that I do this with unconditional love."

"Perhaps," the man drawled. "But you have had thirty-four years living as a human. You will no longer be able to stay in close contact with your human family and friends. The changes, or rather, lack of changes, to your physical form will be noticeable after a while. People will start asking questions. Uncomfortable questions. You may be forced to withdraw from human society or move to another place and start fresh somewhere else. How will you deal with that?"

Shirley chuckled. "Isn't it a shame that when a man fails to age, people credit good genes? When a woman fails to age, we point to plastic surgery?" She gazed at the panel, moving from face to face. God, this crowd was tough to read. It was hard to tell if her responses were having any impact at all. She sobered. "The world has changed. Women and men are aging more slowly. Some can credit that to staying out of the sun and good skincare. Others may point to a healthy diet or regular exercise. These days, humans age chronologically, but it is not always apparent physically.

"However, to respond to your question directly, of course, I will miss my life as a human, at least at first. It's the only life

I have ever known. I have had a good life as a human. A happy one. I suppose when things get tough, I will miss it. But I fully expect the rewards to outweigh the regrets.

"As to family and friends, I see even fewer complications. My family ages young, as they say. My grandmother died at seventy-eight without a single gray hair and a remarkably unlined face. She looked half her age." Shirley smiled. "Maybe she had a little vampire in her."

The panel chuckled.

Shirley continued, "So my relatives won't raise many questions, except in jest, if I stop aging. However, my parents have passed and I have no siblings. I have little contact with my other relatives, only during the holidays, and at weddings and funerals. If my lack of aging becomes a problem, I will just cut back on the events I attend." She smirked. "Besides, there's always plastic surgery. Humans are very quick to assume someone has gone under the knife when they seemingly fail to age. I imagine I will be the subject of all sorts of catty remarks." She shrugged. "I am a female judge, one of the few females in a coven of men. People have gossiped about me since I was appointed. It seems to me after all the sh . . . excuse me, crap, I have been subjected to, I deserve to retain my youthful appearance. A small reward for breaking the glass ceiling."

The man smiled at her. "Thank you for your honesty."

Another vampire coughed, and Shirley turned her attention to him. The man's pure white hair was on the longish side, a bit unkempt, and his glasses seemed to perch perilously on the end of his nose. "And have you discussed our reproduction protocols? Are you willing to propagate?"

Shirley blushed. "Yes, my Lord. It is my most sincere wish to bear Donovan's children. While we would prefer the natural method of reproduction, I understand that may not be possible. So, although the method is somewhat experimental, we have decided to collaborate with a surrogate, vampire, of course. I have preserved some of my human eggs in advance of turning and will preserve more post-transformation. We'll just keep trying until it works. It's not like we have a limited window. We will not be deterred."

"All supervised by our researchers, I presume." The man gazed at her and offered a somewhat awkward smile. "We would prefer the natural method of reproduction, too, but it has never been tried with a recently turned female. It is too great of a risk. However, we are doing everything we can to change that. One day, you may be able to bear children."

Shirley smiled at the man. "That would be amazing." She turned to Donovan. "But the first step is permitting me to marry this man."

The man smiled. "That it is. I have no further questions." He gazed at the other men seated at the table. "Are we ready to vote?"

A handsome vampire dressed in sophisticated clothing, with wavy black hair and flashing green eyes, waved his hand. "Before we vote, I would like to speak." The other men nodded. He stood and strode over to Donovan and put his hand on his shoulder.

"Son, when you were growing up, you would ask for the damnedest things. You wanted a ship to sail to the moon and an impregnable plastic bubble to explore the bottom of the sea. At the time, those things were unheard of. Now they're reality. Then you became a crusader for human rights, something that seemed ludicrous at the time. You championed the poor, then the homeless, the falsely accused, and ultimately, those who bore the weight of human discrimination. There were many times your mother and I looked at one another and raised our eyebrows at this son we had brought into the vampire world.

"However, the only thing that brought us true despair was

your continued dalliances with women, humans and vampires. You seemed content to glide from bed to bed without sanction, never developing a solid relationship, never settling down, never falling in love.

"Until you met a woman who is obviously a match. A true match. A love match. Not only does her beauty and intelligence rival yours, but her heart also appears willing to embrace all of you. Am I troubled that she is human? Of course, I am. We fear what we don't understand. But I also know that of all the vampires in this kingdom, you are the one who is most capable of ensuring that this relationship thrives and survives. You have seamlessly traversed the human world for centuries. You understand their foibles, and because you do, you will be able to guide your partner in the vampire world."

He turned toward the panel. "If it was any other vampire making this request, I would not support it. But this is my son. A man who I raised and have grown to respect. I cannot think of a single reason to deny this request. We are at a crossroads here. Rather than enforcing the status quo, we need to start a new chapter. One that very well may save our kind.

"We need to face facts. We have been frozen in time. Our losses during the pandemic in the twentieth century—the tarnished blood that destroyed the minds of so many, necessitating their demise—were severe and we have not recovered. For some reason, our women have grown barren. Births are almost nonexistent. Also, suicide among vampires is increasing at an alarming rate. We are also seeing a rise in crime and addiction. I have to believe it is because so many feel they have no future. Our problems with procreation aside, this can be a lonely life. Perhaps by permitting one of our purebloods to mate with a human, we can change that. We can admit that it is possible to love a human and for a human to truly love one of us."

He placed a hand on Donovan's then Shirley's shoulder.

"Don't you see? These two represent our future. They are a beacon of light in an otherwise dark and cloudy universe. We are always searching for answers, perhaps this is one of them. We can set guidelines, demand adherence to certain protocols . . . we can make this work. We don't have any other choice.

"Let me cast the first vote. I vote, *aye*."

It had been almost two hours. Shirley stood and began to pace. "What is taking so long?" she mumbled.

Donovan laughed. He reached for Shirley and pulled her onto his lap. "Those vamps are like a bunch of old hens. They dither and dally for the sport of it, not because they necessarily disagree. They will play the devil's advocate. They will dissect every detail. And then they will do it again. Finally, after listening to them run circles around each tiny fact, my father will explode and force a vote. He is the one that keeps them in line."

Shirley frowned. "It's just a simple vote. An aye or nay."

"Except it's really not. First of all, it has to be unanimous or it won't be accepted by our kind. Any dissent will be seen as a wedge between those who disagree with human-vamp mating and those who support it. The opposition will simply ignore the decision."

Shirley's eyes narrowed. "You mean get it reversed?"

"I mean ignore it. If we mate with approval, the Coalition cannot reverse its decision. Still, never say never with a vampire."

"Donovan, speak plainly. What does that mean?"

"It means some will continue to attack us. They could seek our exile or create reasons for prosecution."

Shirley gasped. "But I will no longer be human. I will have been turned, so technically, I will be a vampire. That makes no sense."

"Except you won't be a pureblood. You'll be mixed blood. And while I suspect many of our kind have at least a bit of human in their ancestry, they will hate, simply because your origins are not vampire. It's a form of racism, if you will. Even though you have been turned, to some, even our children will be of mixed blood. Only a unanimous vote will protect us, but even then, we may experience some discrimination."

Shirley emitted a long, shuddering sigh. "Donovan, I am a woman. My intelligence has been questioned my entire life. I understand discrimination. However, I am disappointed that your world is not more enlightened than mine."

Donovan patted her hand. "In that, we are probably more similar than you suspect. In many ways, our society mirrors yours. You heard my father. We have the bad and the ugly, but we also have the good. We never get sick. We rarely die. We possess superhuman strength and mostly, a superior intelligence. While we rarely show emotion, there are exceptions. We are still learning to handle them positively."

Shirley gazed at him. "You're talking about controlling your bites, aren't you?"

Donovan nodded. "At one time, our fangs served two purposes, to defend and to feed. The more civilized among us no longer need to feed, though that is not the case in other parts of the world. Many of our medical advances haven't reached third world countries yet. They still need to feed on a human.

"However, we do have a problem with anger management. Controlling anger and fighting the urge to bite is exceptionally difficult for some vampires. You have to remember, not all are purebloods. Those who were turned come from a broad societal spectrum with varying educations, intellectual capabilities, and emotional health. For many centuries, we enslaved those we felt posed a risk, but the world has changed. What we saw as a protective measure, a way to protect humans from rogue vampires is now construed as a dirty little secret that if exposed, could result in significant repercussions."

Donovan nuzzled Shirley. "If we are to integrate into human society, we must fit in, not stand out. Unfortunately, that's not always easy."

Shirley ran a finger through his hair. "You've always made it look easy."

Donovan snorted. "You should have seen me two centuries ago when I first bumbled my way into the human world. I felt entitled and so superior. I made a lot of stupid mistakes. There was a lot of collateral damage among humans. Without my father's guidance, I would not have survived. Back then, permission was required to live in the human world. Mostly, we were required to remain on the fringes, consorting only with our own kind. I wanted to practice law, but only a human barrister agreed to train me. I suspect the vampires thought me too impulsive. My conduct was monitored closely so I wouldn't reveal my secret, but it is safe to say there were many opportunities to take me out to the woodshed."

Shirley chuckled. "So Donovan was a bad boy?"

He smiled. "More a young man interested in challenging boundaries. I pushed and pushed until someone pushed back."

Shirley smiled. "I wonder if our children will be like that. Always pushing boundaries."

Donovan laughed. "In my limited experience, I expect that to be a given. The smarter the child, the harder they push. We are likely to have children of high intelligence. That's almost a guarantee with a pureblood. Our children will be curious and impulsive and brave. They will test us in ways we never imagined. Isn't that part of the reward of parenting?"

"Actually, it's the reason pureblood vampires hire a governess." Donovan's father emerged from the great hall. He held out his hand to Shirley. "Now, let me formally introduce myself. I am Jonathan Trait, Donovan's father, as you might have gathered." He grinned, "And soon to be your father-in-law. Welcome to the family, my dear."

Shirley squealed. "We are approved? They said yes?"

Jonathan chuckled. "Your marriage has officially been sanctioned by the Vampire Coalition. A unanimous vote. There are some conditions, of course. We can discuss those. But one requirement needs your immediate consent."

Donovan scowled. "What's that?"

"That after you host a human ceremony, you also host one for the Vampire Nation. It is imperative that everyone witness your union, so they understand that it is now acceptable."

Donovan rolled his eyes. "A royal wedding? Ye Gods, Father. You couldn't get them to simply live-stream the human one?" He hugged Shirley with one arm. "My bride might run after being exposed to some of our traditions."

His father waved him off. "I trust your mother will ensure that a certain decorum is maintained. Besides, only the ceremony will be public. All other celebrations will be behind closed doors. Just like our relatives, the British royals." He gazed at Shirley. "Do you agree?"

Shirley blinked, her expression one of confusion. "I agree to two ceremonies, but what is this about royalty?" She pushed against Donovan. "What have you been hiding from me?"

Donovan sighed. "Not hiding, really. I just don't regard myself as a royal, anymore. It is only recognized in the vampire world. To expose ourselves to the human world would be disastrous. I expect we would see a modern version of the Salem witch trials unfold. Besides, because we don't age or die, the process of succession proceeds differently. You agree to sit on the throne for a certain period of years, then you step down. I already served my time. I consider my title honorary only." He took Shirley's face in his hands and kissed her, then he peered at his father. "So, we have their approval?"

His father nodded. "The turning process must be underway before the marriage can occur. The Coalition requires a fifty percent completion rate or five treatments. As you know, that's the point where the vampire blood will begin to spontaneously regenerate. The final treatments are purely maintenance. However, those are the requirements for the vampire union, not the human one. You may host a human wedding at any time." He smirked. "Given your status as a sex symbol, I imagine the humans will be quite interested."

Shirley sniffed. "Well, too bad for them. I don't need a big wedding. I don't need to brag to the world that I bagged a prince or Chicago's hottest lawyer. I am perfectly happy getting married on a beach, with no one but the minister and our witnesses. I couldn't survive two *royal* weddings anyway, no matter how different they are." She nuzzled Donovan's neck. "I say we just do it. Maybe in Lake Geneva. After we announce it, the press and everyone else will lose interest, and we can get on with our lives."

Jonathan Trait offered a slight smile. "I see your future wife is not only beautiful and intelligent, but wise, Donovan. That will serve both of you well in our world. Now I really approve." He sighed. "But I am the one who will have to break it to your mother. You know how she loves throwing extravagant affairs. If your human wedding is low-key, I promise you the vampire ceremony will be over the top."

Donovan laughed. "Which means the wedding will be at least a two-hour affair. She'll bring in that opera singer from Rome and the rock star from New Jersey, a children's choir, and God knows what else. It will be an event."

Shirley giggled. "Let your mother have her fun. Besides, my mother is long gone. I don't have anyone to fuss over me. It's nice that you have someone to fuss over you."

Jonathan Trait chuckled. "Alright then. Prepare for a royal

wedding. On steroids."

# Chapter Twenty: The Turning

Shirley rubbed her arm and sniffed. "Why does everything stink in here?" Her gaze swept Donovan's library, seeking the culprit.

Donovan's mother, Gwendolyn, clapped her hands and laughed in delight. "That means it's working, my dear. Your senses are being heightened, as they should be. Soon you'll be like that old man with Limburger Cheese."

While Shirley appreciated her future-mother-in-law keeping her company when Donovan could not, she did have some odd stories. Shirley cocked an eyebrow. "What? I'm confused."

Gwendolyn giggled. "Oh, you know that old human story, about the old man who fell asleep on a park bench and some kids stuck a chunk of Limburger Cheese under his nose? He woke up and declared, *the whole world stinks?*"

Shirley blinked her eyes, still puzzled. Then she giggled. "Okay, I get it. Limburger Cheese stinks so the old man . . ." She shook her head. "Sorry, I think these infusions are causing brain fog. Sometimes, it's hard to think."

Gwendolyn patted her hand. "Well, you only have one more treatment to go. Then your body will begin to adjust to all the new sensations. I promise you, it will be much better when it's done and your body begins to regenerate vampire blood." She grinned. "Though to me, the human scent is always a bit off-putting. Especially human blood. Since we've moved to plasma pills, we don't have to deal with it anymore. I used to have to wear nose plugs just to feed." She shuddered.

Shirley laughed. "That's reassuring."

A look of horror crossed Gwendolyn's face. "Oh dear, you did not think that I would . . ."

Shirley giggled. "I just meant other vampires wouldn't be tempted. Until I'm turned, that is."

A nurse walked into the room, a chart in her hands. She checked the bag that had held the vampire blood, then removed the pic line that had been inserted into Shirley's arm. When Shirley began to bleed, she turned toward a table that held supplies and grabbed a band-aid. "Sorry, I'm so used to vampire blood coagulating quickly. We don't see many big bleeds. I forgot that you're not one of us yet." She quickly tore open the bandage and fastened it to the cut in Shirley's arm, then she bent the arm up.

Shirley smiled. "You're forgiven. This time." At the nurse's surprised expression, she laughed. "I'm just teasing. It's no problem. I know you don't do many of these."

The nurse frowned.

"Oh, Lauralie, don't get your panties in a bunch," Gwendolyn said. "You're used to terrorizing children. You're not used to adults giving you grief."

Lauralie nodded. "That's true." She half-smiled. "I rarely get an adult vamp to treat. Most know how to take care of wounds themselves. Since they heal so quickly, they usually don't need me. It's the little ones who haven't transitioned yet who need the help." She sighed. "But now that we're likely to have more human patients. I'm going to have to get reacquainted with human medicine. It will be a pain to get up to speed."

Shirley gasped dramatically. "Are you saying I've been a pain?"

Lauralie waggled her eyebrows. "Well, you're human, aren't you? Most humans . . ."

Gwendolyn sighed. "She's a human in the process of turning. Soon she will be one of us. Give it a rest, Lauralie. Not all humans are like the wimps you date."

Lauralie half-smiled. "God, I hope not." She examined Shirley's arm. "Okay, another hour to make sure you don't suffer any side effects, then you're free to go." She left the room.

Gwendolyn gazed at her, concern clouding her eyes. "I hope her comments about humans didn't offend you. I fear not everyone is as tolerant as Donovan, his father, and me. Some oppose mixed marriages because they hate the human race, but to most, they are a curiosity. Lauralie has gotten herself into more than a few pickles with male humans. Unfortunately, she has a thing for motorcycle gangs, and while she enjoys the lax *mores*, she isn't always prepared for the consequences. Some of those men have a thing about ownership and they don't let go easily. More than once she has had to utilize her fangs to escape from a violent situation. Now she has raised a few hackles and one motorcycle gang is starting to ask questions. The Coalition has issued a warning, but I'm not sure she has taken it seriously. If she exposes herself, she endangers all of us. We have no wish to get into a conflict with humans. The number of deaths on their side could not be easily explained."

Shirley nodded. "As a free-loving female, she is accepted. As a free-loving vampire, not so much. Still, I do wonder how all of you have hidden your true selves all these years. It must be frightfully difficult."

Gwendolyn straightened the pleats on her skirt, looking deep in thought. She shrugged. "Not really. Some, like Donovan, are quite skilled at it. Others, like myself and my husband, choose to spend our time alone. When we do mingle, it is with family and friends. There's almost no risk there. As long as Donovan's avocation requires human interaction, he will take that risk."

Shirley studied her future mother-in-law. "I admit one thing puzzles me. Why don't vampires have their own system of justice, you know, lawyers, courts, judges, jails? It seems the most practical way to remove chaos from a society."

Gwendolyn laughed. "We have no need for that in our world. The Coalition is the law. They and they alone mete out justice. And in our world, we have right and wrong, and only two punishments, exile or death. There are no exceptions. No gray areas. That knowledge alone forces people to behave.

"What if you make a mistake? What if you condemn the wrong person?"

Gwendolyn smiled. "Our heightened senses enable us to read a lie. Upon questioning, we know without a doubt whether someone tells the truth or offers a lie. A vampire can't successfully lie to another vampire. It just isn't possible. We don't need juries, witnesses, or trials. A simple question and a simple answer are all it takes to render justice."

Shirley's eyes widened. "That's kind of amazing. If I had that ability, my job would be so much easier."

Gwendolyn allowed a small smile. "With humans, lies are rather blatant. They are always discernable by a vampire. Once you have been fully turned, you will have that same ability. You will know when anyone who comes before you is guilty or innocent. Over time, you will begin to see the futility of a trial. Even after being presented with the evidence and confusing contradictory testimony, the only truth that will shine through is in the defendant's eyes. Humans subscribe to reasonable doubt or compelling evidence. That leaves true justice open to the prejudices of a jury or a judge. That's why mistakes are made. As a vampire, you will never have any doubt."

Shirley groaned. "On second thought, that may make my job a million times harder. I have to adhere to the human system of justice. I have to base my decisions on the evidence presented, not what is in someone's eyes. How can I remain silent when someone's guilt or innocence is so transparent?"

"That's why Donovan's sister handles only appeals. She never sees the convicted. Her decisions are based solely on the law. Her only acquaintance with the accused is a legal brief. It's much less stressful."

An expression of confusion crossed Shirley's face. "I knew Donovan had a sister. I didn't know she was a judge."

Gwendolyn shook her head. "Marilyn is a lot to handle. Ambitious. Ruthless. Totally lacking in manners. I imagine Donovan wanted to keep her under wraps until the wedding so she didn't scare you away."

"Surely she can't be that bad."

"I'm afraid my daughter carries a rather large chip on her shoulder. You see, despite our centuries of experience, the vampire world has not been as quick to recognize women as equals. So many are entrenched in the old ways. Remember, we have lived through hundreds of years where women were second-class citizens. Change is not easy for us. Marilyn has been advocating for a seat on the Coalition. In the human world, she would have succeeded. Vampires are not as liberal, I am afraid. And Marilyn has been like a bull in a china shop. She refuses to see that some men are more susceptible to honey than vinegar. Instead of approaching the subject with grace, she prefers to cast insults and engage in inappropriate behavior."

"I would still enjoy meeting her."

"Beware, Marilyn has you in her sights. She will attempt to convince you to join her on her rampage against the Coalition. She had a chance to make a positive statement when she had Donovan's half-proxy. Like a spoiled child, she ranted and raved when she disagreed with a decision. It was unseemly and quite embarrassing. I know that some humans capitulate under that kind of behavior, but vampires do not. If anything, her histrionics solidified opposition to female members. No one wishes to be exposed to such uncivil behavior on a regular basis." Her smile was tinged with sadness. "Success in the human world has given her a sense of entitlement that has not been earned among vampires. Unless and until she gains the respect of the Coalition, she will not have their ear."

Shirley frowned. "But her brother and father are members. Haven't they provided her with some support?"

Gwen shook her head. "Unfortunately, they must abstain from matters proposed by or about family. Both have advised her how to approach the Coalition, but she has refused to listen. She is her own worst enemy"

"And how do you feel about it. Women's rights, that is?"

"I am perfectly content with my position in the hierarchy. I am respected and treated well. When I have an opinion, my husband listens. He may not agree, but I know he considers my words. We compromise on the big issues, but I have never felt that his opinion is the only one that matters. I feel we are partners in every way. Besides, our laws protect women from abuse and subjugation. We banished slavery well over a century ago. Any mistreatment of women is punished."

Shirley nodded. "So the real issue is the balance of power in governance, not necessarily in the role of women in everyday life."

Gwen rolled her eyes. "I fear the real issue is Marilyn's need to gain access to a club that has denied her membership. No other female vampire has expressed interest. We trust the Coalition to act in our best interests. Until there is a matter of bitter disagreement, we see no reason to rock the boat. Besides, there are always ways to influence the Coalition—with charm and grace. Skills my daughter lacks."

Shirley arched an eyebrow. "So, you and your daughter don't get along?"

Gwen shrugged. "Our approach to life differs, but I love my daughter. However, most of the time, I'm not sure I *like* her." She reached into her bag and pulled out a wedding magazine. "Now, about your wedding, I have a few ideas . . ."

Donovan smiled as he watched workers scurry around the Coalition ballroom, the site for all royal weddings. The large room had been transformed into a winter paradise, resplendent in silver, blue, and gold. His mother had gone all out. It was exactly what the occasion called for. To the uninformed human, it might appear a bit ostentatious, but it was truly fit for a prince and now, his princess.

The ceremony was more than an homage to love. It was also a celebration of continuity. The creation of a new family symbolized hope in a society that experienced few deaths and even fewer births. The prospect of new blood was indeed cause for celebration. A vampire wedding was a ceremony steeped in tradition, yet filled with hope.

"This reminds me of my own wedding." Jonathan Trait clapped Donovan on his shoulder. "Though your mother has added a few more touches. We had a string quartet. She seems to have assembled an orchestra."

Donovan chuckled. "She wanted a gospel choir, but Shirley assured her that was going overboard."

Jonathon Trait smiled. "She also put the kibosh on the horse and carriage, a royal litter, and a throne. Your Shirley does not have a pretentious bone in her body. She allowed your mother a little leeway, but she insisted on simplicity. I am surprised your mother agreed."

"Well, she did allow Mother to bring in a swing band for the reception and the salsa band for the afterparty."

"But she nixed the celebrity chef and insisted on a local one. A human."

Donovan snorted. "Whose memory will be wiped clean as

soon as the celebration ends. He will think he catered a party for Chicago's inner circle, nothing more."

"Well, it's not like we will be flashing our fangs or feasting on humans. Our ceremony will be long and filled with ritual, but to most outsiders, it's a mix of a coronation and an ancient religion. Odd, but nothing extreme." Jonathan removed a gold pocket watch from his vest. "I have been waiting for the physician's report to present to the rest of the Coalition. The wedding can't proceed without a proper license."

Donovan cocked an eyebrow. "Still? I thought that was to be completed this morning."

"The physician wanted to run some tests. He was worried about side effects from the turning."

Donovan paled. "Did he think Shirley ill?"

His father shook his head. "No, nothing like that. I think Shirley reported feeling a little light-headed."

"Maybe I should go to her . . ."

Jonathan grabbed his arm. "Don't you dare. I am under strict orders to keep you away from the bride. Your mother would have my head."

"But if she is ill . . ."

"We would have heard by now."

A messenger rushed into the room carrying a large envelope. He handed it to Jonathan. "From Doctor Mendes, My Lord."

Jonathan bowed stiffly. "Please thank the good doctor for me." The messenger scurried away. He opened the envelope and reviewed the report. When he got to the last page, his eyes grew wide. "Donovan, it seems Shirley had a reason for that lightheadedness."

Donovan gasped. "What is it?"

His father handed him a page and pointed. "Your bride-to-be is pregnant."

Donovan grabbed at the wall, then for a nearby chair. He

felt overwhelmed with emotion. Shakily, he settled onto the chair and rested his head in his hands. "Ye Gods," he muttered. "I'm going to be a father."

The high society matron slowly opened her eyes.

She frowned. The large room was filled with color and flowers. Lots of flowers. How strange. Through her anesthesia fog, she sensed she was not in her own bed.

"She's waking up," a male voice said.

He had a strange accent. French? Dutch? German?

"Finally. Now we can assess her progress. While she healed substantially in her comatose state, we also need to assess whether we managed to save her brain. Brain surgery is always a little dicey."

Okay, she had to be in a hospital. But why did she have brain surgery? There was nothing wrong with her brain. A thought floated through her consciousness. Oh yes, cancer. Had the cancer reached her brain?

"But you did remove all the cancer from her brain, correct?"

The matron moaned. She knew that voice. It was . . . her husband. The man she loved.

"Of course," the other man said. "We believe it was completely successful. Unfortunately, the brain is a very complex organ. When conducting surgery, there is always a chance of damage. The slip of a scalpel, the nudge of a sponge. We can't know the impact until we test her neurological responses."

"And what of her behavior?" her husband asked. "She was hallucinating quite frequently before her collapse."

The matron moaned again. Hallucinations? She didn't recall any hallucinations. All she could remember was the desire to kill. She struggled to hold onto the thought. Who did she want to kill and why? Her eyelids grew heavy. The darkness was closing in. She sighed heavily. Maybe after a nap, she would remember . . .

# You may also enjoy the following from eXtasy Books Inc:

*Martimus*
Seelie Kay

Excerpt

"Why, Cate, you do clean up nice."

Cate took a sip of her martini and studied the pasty-faced man over the rim of her glass. "Why, thank you, Charles." She paused. "Tell me, how is Jackie? What is she, about four months along now?"

Charles Wright shrugged. "I guess. I haven't seen her in a while. We're sort of taking a break."

Cate studied him. His flat brown hair framed a lackluster face. His eyes were a bit too close together, his nose unattractively broad. Not someone she would enjoy waking up next to every morning, though Jackie was no beauty either. Cate tapped his arm with her blood-red nails. "Take my advice, Charles. Marry that girl before she takes off with your child, then demands your liver in exchange for visitation rights." Cate cocked an eyebrow. "By the way, have you seen Elise Ellis? I was supposed to meet her here, and I can't find her anywhere."

Charles cast Cate a speculative glance. "I was not aware

you were even acquainted." His eyes narrowed. "And why would you be asking me about Elise anyway? Have you heard something about us? Oh God, please tell me there are not any rumors going around about us. They simply are not true. If Jackie hears about this . . ."

Cate tried not to chuckle. Charles seemed quite panicked. Obviously, he and Elise had been up to something. Charles had a reputation for loving and leaving 'em, which was why, when learning of her pregnancy, Jackie had quickly fastened a legal noose around his neck. Poor Charles was still struggling to breathe. If Jackie learned of any outside dalliances, she was sure to tighten that noose ever more firmly. Jackie expected Charles to marry her. Period. Charles had already signed a support agreement that would permit Jackie to live like royalty for the rest of her life, but she was holding out on custody and visitation rights until Charles put a ring on her finger. Good heavens, Jackie was already four months along. If they waited much longer to marry, no one would believe that the child had arrived prematurely.

Cate tittered and patted Charles on the arm. "No need to panic, darling. I've heard nothing. I was merely inquiring about Elise because we were supposed to meet up." Cate had no such plans, she simply wanted to know where Elise was. She turned and moved to a group of young men gathered in a corner.

The rowdy discussion stopped as she approached. "Why, Cookie" one man drawled. "You are a sight for sore eyes. Where have you been hiding those spectacular tits?"

Cate fought the desire to slug the obnoxious cur. Cookie was a childhood nickname and she had hated it. In a flirtatious tone, she replied, "Archie, I'm surprised you even noticed." Her expression turned sly. "Word is that you are head over heels for Elena Bosworth. Should I expect a wedding invitation?"

Archie groaned. "Jesus, show a little affection for a chit and the old ball and chain gets hauled out of the closet. I am too young for a life sentence." His friends nodded. He continued, "Besides, word is that she has set her sights on old Fuzzy Winston." He placed a finger on the side of his nose and sniffed. "Apparently, he keeps her quite happy."

Cate arched an eyebrow. "Where is the Fuzz, anyway? I haven't seen him in weeks. He rarely misses a party."

Archie shrugged. "Who knows? Maybe Elena has him hog-tied to her bed. She did display some unattractive dominant traits." He shuddered. "My future wife will know who wields the whip, and it won't be her."

The other men murmured their assent.

Cate rolled her eyes. Sometimes, it was difficult to be polite to Archie. He wore his chauvinism on his sleeve. And his lack of concern for a man he called a friend was troubling. Fuzzy Winston had been missing for several months. Archie wasn't even a little concerned.

Strong arms circled Cate's waist and moist lips nuzzled her neck. "Let's blow this pop stand and have some real fun, babe," crooned a mellow baritone. A hand removed the drink from her hand and placed it on the tray of a passing waiter. "Dance with me."

Cate turned and stared up into Warren Hazelton's ice-blue eyes. She gave him a sweet smile. "I thought you'd never ask." The tall, solidly built former U.S. Navy Seal pulled her onto the dance floor and swept her into a waltz. He held her body tightly against his. Through her thick fake eyelashes, Cate peered up at him. "Aren't you supposed to be guarding Hope?"

"I convinced Sibley to trade places. He's watching Hope while I'm watching you. No offense to the pipsqueak, but I'd much rather be watching you!" He grinned. "Besides, there are so many bodyguards in this room that if anyone made a move on the sweet princess, they'd be riddled with bullets before they could pull a weapon. And as Hope pointed out, my presence intimidates. She said she can't do her job with me hulking around. So I'm giving her a little space." He chuckled.

"Since Hope was kidnapped right out from under from her husband's nose, Tom's been more vigilant, too. Trust me, she's well protected."

Cate smiled. "Well, perhaps she'll have better luck than me. The only rumors I could catch are that Charles Wright carries defective condoms and may have dallied with Elise Ellis in the past, and Fuzzy Winston may have been compromised by the lovely Elena Bosworth. No one seems at all concerned that he has not been seen for almost three months." She reached up and stroked his short platinum hair, affection overwhelming her heart. God, this man made her positively giddy. "We are not dealing with the brightest bulbs in the chandelier here, but you'd think they would be questioning the absence of their friends."

"You know how this group is, friendship is fickle. One week they're your bestie, the next they've never heard of you." Warren pulled away from Cate and his gaze swept her body. "By the way, this dress would force even the most proper gentleman to indulge in a little ungentlemanly behavior. Really, Cate, it's more skin than fabric. You don't leave much to the imagination." He brushed his hand across her bare back. "I would reveal my deepest, darkest secrets for a peek under this thing. It's worse than running a boink me ad during the Superbowl." He pulled her closer to him, trailing kisses from her ear to her neck. "No. Subtlety. At. All."

"Warren, darling, trying to mark your territory?"

His hand slid down her half-naked body and rested just above the curve of her ass. Warren kissed her lightly. "Most definitely."

Cate frowned. This thing with Warren was getting a little confusing. Sure, members of the Agency tended to couple up. When you worked in covert operations, it was just easier. However, Cate was a honeypot—the agent assigned to romance, dazzle, and sometimes seduce persons of interest. She used sex to wring the truth from informants, suspects, traitors, and outright villains. It was her job to appear footloose and fancy-free, not enamored with a gorgeous hunk of man-flesh.

"Down, boy," she whispered. "We're working tonight. Save the romance for our bedroom."

Her team had been assigned to find a group of young socialites who had gone off the grid. All of the missing were linked to prominent politicians or government leaders, making them high-value targets. They could have been taken for ransom, to force their parents into providing unsavory political favors, or other questionable purposes. Because no one had been able to find them, their disappearance remained a mystery. And because her fellow socialites showed so little interest, no one seemed compelled to launch a search. It wasn't until a former Vice-President's daughter went AWOL that the Agency had been called in.

The Agency's mission was twofold. First, they were to determine how many highly connected socialites were missing. The best way to do that was to mingle and focus in on the rumor mill. This circle fed on gossip. If there was a rumor to be had, they knew about it. Second, every member of the team had similar familial connections—their parents all served in positions of influence and power. Conceivably, they were targets as well. If they brought enough attention to themselves, perhaps they could attract the interest of those who had a hand in the disappearances. At the moment, all they had was a lot of speculation and very few facts. They didn't even know if the disappearances were related.

Cate gazed at Warren. "It's hard enough to get these people to talk. Hope's right, you're intimidating. I can't have you hanging around, acting like you're going to go all caveman on anyone who looks twice at me. You need to chill out and fade into the background."

Warren scoffed. "None of these people can see past that scandalous dress you're wearing. Besides, given your reputation, I'm just going to be seen as another one of your conquests." He cocked an eyebrow. "Hopefully, not the one with the leaky condoms."

Cate giggled. "Warren, darling, I think you just called me a slut."

Warren chuckled. "No. I'm merely complimenting your skills as an actress. I know you're not promiscuous. Heck, it took three months to get you into my bed, and I put in maximum effort. If you want to behave like a slut in our bedroom, you won't find me complaining."

Cate slapped at him and giggled. "You are a dirty old man, Warren Hazelton." She blew him a kiss and said sweetly, "Later, sailor." Then she walked away, putting an extra swing in her step—just for Warren's benefit.

# About the Author

Seelie Kay writes about lawyers in love, sometimes with a dash of kink.

Writing under a nom de plume, the former lawyer and journalist draws her stories from more than 30 years in the legal world. Seelie's wicked pen has resulted in eighteen works of fiction, including the **Kinky Briefs** series, **The Feisty Lawyers** series, **The Garage Dweller**, **A Touchdown to Remember**, **The President's Wife, The President's Daughter, Seizing Hope**, **The White House Wedding, The Last Christmas**, as well as the romance anthology, **Pieces of Us**.

When not spinning romantic tales, Seelie ghostwrites nonfiction for lawyers and other professionals. Currently, she resides in a bucolic exurb outside Milwaukee, WI, where she shares a home with her son and enjoys opera, the Green Bay Packers, gourmet cooking, organic gardening, and an occasional bottle of red wine.

Seelie is an MS warrior and ruthlessly battles the disease on a daily basis. Her message to those diagnosed with MS: Never give up. You define MS, it does not define you!

Seelie can be reached at www.seeliekay.com, www.seeliekay.blogspot.com, or on Twitter or Facebook.

www.ingramcontent.com/pod-product-compliance
Lightning Source LLC
LaVergne TN
LVHW050638100826
845148LV00011B/1899

*9781487431266*